Swe

Indigo Bay Sweet Romance Series

Danielle Stewart

Copyright

An original work of Danielle Stewart

Cover Designed by Najla Qamber Designs
www.najlaqamberdesigns.com

ISBN-13: 978-1546771470

ISBN-10: 1546771476

Sweet Rendezvous

On her last tank of gas Elaine Mathews drives South. Spontaneity had never been her strength, but there was something about being publicly fired that had a way of changing things. An empty bank account, broken heart, and enough humiliation to last a life time was all Elaine could claim as her own. Her car choked to a stop in the quiet beach town of Indigo Bay and all she could do was sit on the curb and wait for the sun to set on her misery.

Davis Mills has a routine. Wake. Work. Eat. Sleep. Repeat. It hadn't always been that way. He'd left indigo bay once and returned a broken man. Now he kept his dreams small and his schedule tight. If there was no room in his life for anything new then he'd never repeat his mistakes.

When fate has them, quite literally colliding Elaine and Davis are faced with an important question. Can you live a full life if you never take a risk? Or is life made up of every mistake, miracle and chance that comes with being in love?

Indigo Bay Romance Series

The Indigo Bay world has been written so readers can dive in anywhere they want in the series without missing a beat. Read one or read all six. They're sweet and delicous treats.

Sweet Dreams by Stacy Claflin

Sweet Matchmaker by Jean Oram

Sweet Sunrise by Kay Correll

Sweet Illusions by Jeanette Lewis

Sweet Regrets by Jennifer Peel

Sweet Rendezvous by Danielle Stewart

Chapter One

The passing street lights were reduced to blurry orbs, obscured by the tears in Elaine's eyes. She wasn't entirely sure when the sun had set. Without her noticing, day had been devoured by dusk. Dusk was now entirely consumed by the night's pitch-black darkness. Her sleek black stilettoes were somewhere a mile or so behind her, kicked off when the blisters became unbearable. That pain was gone now. Numbness had taken over. She'd long since stopped feeling the jagged pinch of rocks against the soles of her feet. There was no longer any sensation as she stumbled step by step farther from all she was attempting to outrun.

Using the sleeve of her dusty fitted white button-up shirt, she cleared her eyes and tried to focus on the mirage-like scene coming into view. Elaine knew her legs would not carry her much longer. At least three miles back her car had sputtered to a stop, sucking the fumes of the last gallon of gas in the tank. Whatever salvation was up ahead, she'd have to allow it to swallow her up.

As she inched closer to civilization her heart was lulled by the rhythmic drumming of waves pummeling the sand over the dunes she passed. The street sign read Seaside Blvd., and something about being by the ocean calmed her. The salt in the air was so heavy she could taste it on her lips. It was the closest thing to food she'd had since the previous night. When buildings and lights finally folded in around her, she felt the drag of her feet grow more pronounced. The ability to lift them was fleeting as she settled in on a curb lit by the neon lights of a hardware store. It looked like it had been closed for hours. Everything on the street was still, eerily so, considering what every corner in New York City looked like this time of night.

Forward motion had been her only goal for the last fourteen hours. *Move. Keep moving.* Now that she'd finally stopped, the difficult task of taking inventory of the journey's toll began. Her feet were stained black with dirt. The light behind her cast a shadow on the sidewalk, showing how frazzled and unkempt her normally sleek blonde hair had become. The gray pencil skirt she'd slid into early that morning was now covered in dirt and shimmied too far up her body to be comfortable.

"Ma'am?" A voice burst into her life like an intruder kicking down the door to her mind. "Ma'am are you all right?"

"Fine," she answered out of habit. "I'm fine." A lesson learned many years ago. Rule number one for a woman in a male-dominated business. If you were less than fine, there was some womanly reason why. If you were mad, you were hormonal. If you were hurt, you were too sensitive. "I'm fine," she repeated, surprised by how raspy and tired her voice sounded.

"Did you have car trouble?" the figure looming over her asked, and finally she turned her eyes up and blinked until he was in focus. "My name is Davis. I can call a tow if you need it."

"Yes," she answered, nodding and patting her hair, fruitlessly trying to tame it. The man was like a giant, his broad shoulders fighting a war against his snug flannel shirt, looking like they were about to win. Sandy blond hair dipped across his forehead and nearly covered his eyes, until he wrangled it back with a flip of his hand.

"Do you need a tow?" he asked again, speaking slowly enough for her to realize he wasn't sure she was sane. How could she blame him? She was a sight.

"No, the car is a few miles back. I'm leaving it there. I don't need a tow." She tried to shift her skirt over her scraped knees. She'd fallen somewhere along the way and banged them up.

"You're leaving your car back there?" he asked, gesturing with his hand the way she'd come. "Is it just on the side of the road or something?"

"I don't need it anymore. I live here now." She shrugged, crossing her legs at the ankle, as though suddenly remembering she was a lady, and even when hitting rock bottom she should act like it.

"You live in Indigo Bay now?" he asked, arching one of his thick brows at her quizzically.

"Indigo Bay?" she asked, looking up and down the small street as though she were assessing the whole scene.

"Yes, that's where you are. You said you live here now?" He was nervously wringing his hands, moving them like a load of laundry repeatedly tumbling in the dryer.

She laughed in a breathy way as though he were the one being ridiculous. "I live here now," she said, patting the hard cement below her. "I live on this curb."

"Oh," he said, nodding as though he could officially deem her insane now. "I see. Well, it's going to rain so you may want to rethink your new living arrangements. It doesn't look like you have much shelter."

"It's not going to rain," she said, looking up at the dark night sky. "It's a perfectly nice night. I'll be fine, thank you. Dave, was it?"

"Davis," he corrected, unwavering in his concern. "And I've lived here my whole life. When the air smells like this, and the wind changes so quick, there's rain coming."

Elaine sniffed at the air and looked at him curiously. "Really? I don't smell anything."

"My bum shoulder starts aching too," he said, jutting his chin out confidently. Her eyes narrowed as she scanned his face until he faltered into a smile. "Plus they just said it on the radio." If his smile wasn't so damn magnetic, she'd probably yell at him for being smug. He was interrupting a perfectly good mental breakdown here.

"I'll be just fine. Thank you for stopping." She folded her arms across her chest and pretended to be interested in the empty street. No matter what she wouldn't look at him again. That would make it clear she wanted him gone.

"I can't leave you here," Davis apologized. "It's late. You're alone. Clearly you've had a rough day. I really don't want to sit on that curb next to you in the rain, so maybe I can take you somewhere."

"You say it like it's some kind of law you have to help me," she scoffed. "I lived in New York City. I can assure you that you are under no legal obligation to stop and help anyone. I once saw a guy texting while he crossed the street. He got hit by a cab and about six people stepped right over him and his broken leg without even noticing. So as much as I appreciate the charming southern guy act, I don't need it."

"There's a lot to unpack there," Davis said, rubbing his chin thoughtfully. "But the only thing you should know is the curb that's now your house, it's in Indigo Bay. People here don't step over anyone. It might not be law, but I can promise you there are about ten old ladies at the church that would beat me within in an inch of my life if they heard I left you out here. It would be a flurry of umbrellas and oversized handbags stuffed with hard candies. Do me a favor and save me that pain. I'll give you a lift to the cottages. My buddy Dallas owns them. I can get him on the phone even at this late hour. I'm sure he can set you up with something. I think he's close to full up, but he's always got something he can work out."

"I can't afford that," Elaine said, clearing her throat. Somehow that admission was harder for her than being seen in her disheveled state.

"Well there's a motel at the back side of the property. Those rooms are cheaper. Like I said, I don't know what they'll have open."

"I don't have any money," she explained. "I left

without my wallet. I don't have my credit cards, my driver's license. Nothing."

"You left in a hurry?" he asked, looking thoroughly concerned now. Any levity he'd been trying to interject was gone. "Are you in some kind of danger?" He looked up and down the street as though the threat might be imminent.

"No." She laughed. "Nothing that exciting. I don't want to talk about it. I just want to sit here and—" It suddenly dawned on her that she couldn't finish that sentence. What exactly did she want to come next?

"Not much of a planner are you?" Davis asked, sitting down next to her with a loud huff. "So you live on this curb now, and that's all you know." A rumble of thunder boomed in the distance.

"You're not leaving are you?" she asked, giving him a sideways look filled with annoyance. In truth she felt a little relieved to have some company.

"I'll take you over to see Caroline. She'll know how to sort this out. She owns a coffee shop down the way. It's late, and they're closed now. It's past ten o'clock but she stays late."

"It's past ten at night?" Elaine asked, stunned by how long she'd been traveling. "It's been a long day."

"She'll know what to do," Davis promised as he stood and extended a hand for her to take. Lightning lit the sky behind him, and she felt the charge jolt her heart.

"You seem pretty sure about that," Elaine sighed, getting reluctantly to her feet. "Maybe you didn't get a good enough look at me. I have no shoes. Did you notice that?"

"I noticed everything," Davis replied as they walked down the silent street with him just a half step ahead.

"What state am I in?" Elaine asked, suddenly realizing she'd lost track somewhere along the way.

"South Carolina," Davis said tentatively. Clearly his level of concern for her stability continued to grow like snow piling up in a blizzard. "You really don't know where you are?"

"I didn't care where I ended up," Elaine admitted, wincing as a rock caught the soft spot of her heel. "I only cared I wasn't where I started this morning."

"You need shoes," he said, watching her try to dodge anything that might hurt her feet. "Hop on my back," he said, gesturing for her to climb up.

"That's ridiculous. I'm not getting a piggy back ride. I'm a grown woman."

"You know who usually gets piggy back rides? Toddlers. And you know what you have in common with a toddler right now? A lot. You have no money. No shoes. You look overtired and cranky. Now get on."

He was stopped in front of her, and she knew trying to get by would be pointless. Plus her feet were throbbing and scraped. Davis crouched down a few inches lower, and she hopped on. Her arms looped around his neck, and his hands slipped under her legs to hold her up. "If you say I'm heavier than I look, I'm going to hop down and make you regret it."

"You're like a feather," he said, pretending to be

serious. “I hardly know you’re here at all.”

“I’ll pretend you didn’t grunt when I first got on,” she said, resting her tired chin down on him.

“How exactly did you end up here?” he asked, as he moved effortlessly down the street, even with her weight on him.

“It’s not that complicated. Basically I got in the car with nothing but a little cash in my pocket. I drove south, stopping to fill the tank once with the money I had. Kept driving until the car ran out of gas and my money was gone. Then I walked until I couldn’t walk anymore.”

“Very uncomplicated,” Davis agreed sarcastically. “As clear as mud. The good news is the light is on at Sweet Caroline’s. She must still be there.” He let her down, and she missed their closeness the second her feet hit the pavement.

“I’m suddenly regretting getting off my curb,” Elaine admitted, hesitating at the door step to the café. She’d have to face another stranger during what could only be described as her rock bottom.

“Caroline doesn’t judge,” Davis offered, but Elaine knew better than that. Everyone judged. Everyone looked out for themselves. “I’m sure she can help.”

“I’m sure she can’t,” Elaine sighed as he pulled open the door. “I thought you said they were closed? Why is the door unlocked?”

“Before you get your mail forwarded to your new curb, you’re going to have quite a bit to learn about Indigo Bay.” Davis laughed. “This is not New York.”

Elaine looked around the quaint café and felt a

wash of relief as she heard his words. “This is not New York,” she repeated. “Thank goodness for that.”

Chapter Two

"Boy, you know those coffee pots are off," a gentle southern voice called out to them. "If you think you're going to sweet talk me into feeding you right now—" She stopped abruptly as she got close enough to see Elaine. Davis knew Caroline was the right person to help, but it didn't mean this wouldn't get weird for a little while first.

"This is Elaine," he stuttered out. "She had car trouble."

"Did the car try to eat you?" Caroline asked, scanning the girl like an X-ray machine.

"It's a long story," Elaine offered, but Caroline looked far from convinced. "I'm kind of stranded here. I don't have anything. No money or clothes."

"Isn't that a pickle?" Caroline sighed. "Well you came to the right place. Are you hungry?"

"I am, but you just said . . . I mean it sounded like a headache to have to get food out."

Caroline laughed in the way only she could. It was smooth like jazz, rising and falling in all the perfect spots. Unpredictable, a little frantic but perfect. "That was only for Davis. He knows better. You're new around here, and you're clearly in need. It's my pleasure to fill your belly. Have a seat over there, and I'll bring you out something."

"I should get going," Davis said, tired from a

long day's work and nervous Elaine could end up in tears any moment. Something he was wholly unprepared to deal with.

"No way," Caroline ordered, pointing at the nearest booth. "You aren't off the hook. This young lady is going to need a place to stay tonight."

"I know," Davis said, his face twisting with confusion. "That's why I brought her to you."

"This is a café, not a hotel. I don't have any room at my place. You on the other hand have a bunch of dusty old rooms at your house."

"She can't stay with me," Davis shot back quickly. "What would Lucille say about a scandalous, juicy rumor that I've got a strange woman sleeping at my place?"

"Since when do you care what the town gossip has to say about you? If you were really worried about Lucille, I'd think you'd have indulged her and taken her up on one of those blind dates she's always needling you to go on." She turned to Elaine. "Now listen here, I'm going to feed you; I have a pair of sandals you can wear, and in the light of day I'll be happy to help you figure out what you need. But it's late, and I don't have any space for you. Davis will put you up for one night."

"I don't even know him," Elaine whispered and for the first time it struck Davis how intimidating his arrival might have been. How intrusive, maybe even scary, his insisting might have seemed.

"Darling, if you drew a circle a thousand miles around Indigo Bay, there wouldn't be a man I'd trust more than Davis Mills. He's an honorable man of his word and a true gentleman to his core. You don't need to know him; I know him enough for both of us. Now"—Caroline flipped a dish towel over her shoulder and headed for the back of the café—"let me get you fed and on your way."

"I can pay for a cabin for you," Davis said, fishing his phone from his pocket. "I'll call Dallas and set it up." But the phone only rang and rang until Dallas's voice mail picked up. "He must be sleeping."

"I'll be fine," she said, swallowing so hard her throat bobbed up and down with emotion. "I got myself into this mess. I'm not your responsibility."

"I highly doubt you got yourself into this mess," Davis challenged, dancing the line between respecting her privacy and needing to know what could have possibly transpired to make her run so far so fast. No one just got in their car and ran away from their life unless something serious had happened.

"You don't give me enough credit." She laughed. "I can screw things up pretty bad. That might be another reason you don't want to get too mixed up in this."

"Maybe I should have kept driving tonight when I saw you sitting on that curb," he said flatly, and he watched her face fall a little before she remembered to look tough. "But then I wouldn't be sitting here about to eat one of the most delicious desserts this side of the Mason-Dixon line. Silver linings can come in the form of cobbler."

"The best cobbler in the world might not make up for the trouble that follows me everywhere. I promise I'll sort this out and be on my way tomorrow.

I'll get the bank to mail me a new credit card. I'll put more gas in the car and keep driving."

"You do know if you drive south long enough you run out of road. Unless that car turns into a submarine, you might need a new plan."

"I'll figure it out." She shrugged, her finger tracing nervously along the mosaic tile pattern on the table.

"I don't know what you're running from or why you needed to," Davis said gently, "but what I do know is Indigo Bay is the perfect place to hide out. You're safe here."

"All right," Caroline sang loudly as she balanced two plates on a tray, "sandwiches are the best I can do this time of night. And you know there's cobbler too so don't be giving me those eyes, Davis."

"Yes ma'am," Davis said, biting his lip and dipping his head apologetically. "I should have known better."

"I have a pair of sandals here for you . . . What's your name?"

"Oh gosh," Davis said, the realization hitting him like a punch in the jaw. "I never asked your name."

"Elaine," she whispered as though she was sorry to give up the anonymity. "Thank you so much for the food and the sandals. I'll get money sorted out in the morning and come back to pay you."

"No need," Caroline said, waving the idea off like it was a bothersome fly buzzing by her head. "Davis here will cover you."

"I will?" Davis asked, furrowing his brows playfully.

"Of course you will because this is the closest thing that resembles a date that you've been on in over four years. That means you've got plenty of money saved up to spend a little on a pretty girl's dinner."

"Four years?" Elaine asked in a hushed voice as Caroline hurried off. "You haven't been on a date in four years? That's kind of sad."

"Remind me to get you some window cleaner," Davis said, cutting his sandwich in half. "I want to make sure you can see from your glass house when you start throwing rocks at me."

"Noted," Elaine said, finally cracking a smile. The dim light of the café barely lit her face, but he could see a spark. Looking past the red rims of her eyes that had been crying too long, he could see the bright ice blue sparkle he'd missed. Her features were delicate, appearing more fragile from the shadow cast from the pain. "I should be the last one judging anyone right now."

"Are you going to eat?" he asked, gesturing with his chin at her untouched plate of food. "That chicken salad is best in the county. Five years running actually."

She laughed, looking down at the sandwich as if it were a wild animal about to pounce. "I haven't had this many calories on my plate since freshmen year of high school. "I almost forget what real mayonnaise tastes like."

He pushed the plate closer to her. "Heaven," he said, making a funny face at her. "It tastes like pure heaven."

Chapter Three

Davis was right. That sandwich was the best thing she'd eaten in a very long time. Lettuce wraps and kale smoothies could not compete with what they'd just been served. She'd have to run a marathon tomorrow to make up for the cobbler, but it was worth it. Now as they were riding in his truck, her head was pressed to the glass of the side window as she stared at the sky. "Still predicting rain?"

"It might rain. Mostly, I was just trying to get you off that curb," he admitted, his eyes focused intensely on the road. "That hardware store you were loitering in front of belongs to my friends. I didn't want you scaring off their customers come morning."

"So you're a liar?" she challenged, a giggle in her voice. "Miss Caroline said you were the best man around for miles. Maybe she doesn't know you that well."

"She knows me plenty." He shrugged, looking unaffected by her accusation. As a matter of fact, very little seemed to rattle him. "Everyone knows everyone in Indigo Bay. But I practically grew up in her house. Her son Dallas is my best friend. My dad's in the military. He moved around a lot, and I stayed behind. She and Dallas are family to me."

"That's nice," she breathed out, watching the sleepy town blow by in her peripheral vision. "No one has probably noticed I'm gone yet."

"You don't have anyone in New York?" he asked, seeming to force himself not to look over at her. "No family?"

"No," she said just above a whisper. "My family moved to Europe when I was nineteen. My dad is a businessman, and he got in some trouble. Moving was the way out for him."

"You didn't go?"

"I was in college. I had my whole life planned. Letting his mistakes take that plan from me was not going to happen." It seemed silly now. Her dreams hadn't panned out at all. Maybe drinking wine and eating pasta in Italy with her parents would have been the right choice.

"What do you do for a living?" he probed as he turned down a quiet sand-covered road that looked more beach than street.

"I don't want to talk about that." Her reply was curt. "It's not important. I don't have that job anymore. I'm going to have a new job tomorrow."

"Tomorrow?" he asked, sounding unconvinced. "I thought you were getting the car fueled up and driving."

"I changed my mind. You were right. I'll eventually run out of road anyway. If Indigo Bay is so safe, maybe I should just stay. There must be jobs here. I can do anything. I'm a hard worker. I always have been. Is anyone hiring that you know of?"

"You're going to get a job in Indigo Bay? I don't think there is anything here for you." His laugh was too condescending for her to ignore.

"What's that's supposed to mean? You don't think I'm employable?"

"Your outfit is more expensive than a month's pay for any jobs here. Indigo Bay isn't exactly going to be your speed. I'm sure you'll wake up refreshed tomorrow and decide New York is the place you belong."

"You think all I care about is money?" she asked, as he parked the truck in front of a shockingly bright purple cabin. "That I'm some snobby brat from New York who doesn't belong in your idyllic little beach town?"

"That's not what I meant," he said, tossing his arms up in exasperation. "I just meant—"

"I want to walk the beach," she explained, slamming the door and charging over the dune toward the ocean. It wasn't because Davis was wrong, it was more likely he was right, and she'd fail here too. Some nights you weren't looking for reality. You weren't looking for the truth.

"Wait," he called from behind her, but she didn't slow down. "Hold up for a second. It's dark. It's late. Those dunes are steep. Just get some sleep and forget what I said."

"I'm fine," she yelled back at him as she picked up her pace toward the crashing waves. The sand on the dunes began to give way and she landed on her butt, sliding the rest of the way down.

"See," he shouted. "You're going to break your neck. Just come in the house. I shouldn't have said anything."

"I can sleep in the sand. I want to be alone.

Please, forget you invited me in. I appreciate that you're being nice, but I don't deserve it any more than I want it. It's a beautiful night; let me crash here."

"Fine," he yelled back, a bite of annoyance finally filling his voice. She'd wondered when he would tire of this nonsense, and now she had her answer. "Sleep on the beach. I'm not going to force you to do something you don't want to. Just don't be pissed at me when—"

"When what?" she asked, tossing her arms up in the air as the tears started to fall. "What could possibly be worse than what's already happened? At least I'm under the stars. At least I can hear the waves. What could be worse than the mess I'm in?"

"I have no idea because I don't know what happened to make you run away in the first place? Did your trust fund dip under a million dollars? Did you not get your participation trophy? Maybe you failed at something, and it feels like the end of the world when really it's probably no big deal at all." He was shouting now, throwing his hands up as he spoke from the top of the dunes. "I'm sorry your temper tantrum took you so far from home."

"You don't know anything, Davis." Tears soaked her cheeks. "If you did," she sputtered, "you'd be damn sorry right now. Just leave me alone. Please."

"Elaine," he said, forcing control into his words, "I'm tired. It's been a long weird day, and I think you should come in and go to sleep. You can be pissed at me in there."

"I'm sleeping here," she said, flopping onto the

sand and pulling her knees to her chest, trying to shrink herself down to nothing.

"Your choice," Davis grunted, heading back toward the purple cottage. "In the morning I'll have Miss Caroline send someone for you. Put some gas in your car and keep driving."

"Fine," she yelled, resting her chin on her knees and blinking the tears away. A moment later she heard a squeaky door pulled open and then slammed shut. Lights in the cabin came on and some random banging could be heard between the crashing of the waves. Sleeping on the beach would be just what she needed. The sand was soft. The waves were there to lull her to sleep and . . .

A crack of thunder shook her ribcage and a shock of lightning made her heart skip a beat. The sky came alive with silver drops of rain as though a faucet had suddenly been turned on. "No," she said, closing her eyes and letting the rain hit the back of her neck as she dipped her head low in defeat. Her clothes were soaked through in seconds. Her hair matted to her face. "I can't," she choked out. "I can't deal with this."

"You can," a voice said from behind her. "Come on." Davis reached his hand down but she refused to take it. This guy had been a perfect gentlemen, and she'd done nothing but make the situation worse again and again.

"I'm a mess," she stammered. "I can't do this, Davis."

He dropped to his knees in the sand next to her. She saw his shirt was soaked through as she blinked away the rain. She opened her mouth to protest, but he reached over and looped her arm around his neck. Scooping her up from behind her knees, he lifted her effortlessly and stood up. Carrying her through the sand and up the dunes, he never grimaced with effort. She knew she should apologize. Protest. Insist she could walk. But she wasn't sure she could. Instead Elaine rested her head on his soaked shirt and sobbed as he used his foot to push open the cottage door.

"It's all right," he said, sitting on the couch, keeping her in his lap. "You're all right."

"I can't breathe," she gasped.

"You can," he said, calmly. "You have to. Because I don't know CPR, and if you die here I'll never be able to sell this place. Once people know a girl died here the selling price tanks. Ghosts are a real concern for homebuyers."

She hiccupped out a laugh and fought to fill her lungs with air. "I'm all right. I'm sorry. I'm so sorry for all of this," she whispered against the soft skin of his neck.

"Don't be," he said, clearing his throat and shifting her to the couch as he stood abruptly. "I shouldn't have shouted at you. I don't know your story. It's been a long day. There's a room at the end of the hall. There's plenty of clothes back there that should fit you."

"Umm," she said, leaning so she could see down the hallway. "There are?"

"My room's upstairs. If you need anything, just knock." He shuffled out of the room, his eyes never hitting hers again. A door closed abruptly, and the house fell perfectly silent.

Lightning and a crack of thunder struck all at once and Elaine's hand flew to her heart, fluttering with nerves. She'd been so busy shredding her life to pieces that she'd somehow missed the perfect horror movie scenario she'd walked into. A strange man who turned up out of nowhere. A thunderstorm. And a mysterious bedroom full of women's clothes.

The only silver lining: if she was going to die tonight at least she'd gotten that cobbler.

Chapter Four

Davis stared up at the ceiling as ribbons of sunlight cut through his blinds and fought to light his tiny room. *Damn that beautiful woman.* Damn her tears. Damn the rain. He'd had years perfecting the art of being alone. He'd learned exactly how many times you had to break plans before the invitations stopped coming. He could dodge the prospect of a blind date like a pro. But tonight he blew it. The second he pulled Elaine into his arms he knew something had shifted. A door he'd locked and barricaded years ago had been kicked wide open, and Elaine was walking right in.

His best bet this morning would be a well drafted note pinned to the fridge and a quick exit before she woke up. But first he'd need a shower because he'd be useless all day if the smell of her shampoo wasn't washed off his neck.

Elaine had such a rough night he thought she'd be sleeping in. So after his shower he hustled down the stairs and searched his desk for a piece of paper to leave her a note.

"You have no food here." Her tiny voice filled his ears, and he spun around too quickly, trying unsuccessfully to look natural. "Sorry, did I scare you?" she asked, looking apologetic.

"No," he lied. "I just figured you'd be sleeping

in. Sorry though, you're right, I don't have any food."

"What do you eat usually?" she asked, and he noticed a fidgetiness to her this morning. She'd gotten herself ready and looked far more put together, but something was still off.

"I grab coffee at Caroline's before I start work. I never order it, but she always puts a muffin or something in a bag for me. It's been going on that way for years."

"What do you do for work?"

"I'm a boat mechanic," Davis answered, making his way to the kitchen as she followed behind, clearing her throat nervously. "Do you have a lot more questions for me because, even though I might have seemed like it last night, I'm not really a chatty guy? Especially in the morning."

"Just one question," she said, backing up a few steps and nibbling on her lip nervously. "Whose clothes are these, and why do you have them?" She held the hem of the soft pink and blue plaid button-up shirt away from her skin as if it might be toxic. "Dead wife killed tragically and your broken heart hasn't allowed you to part with her things? Maybe it belongs to victims of your homicidal rampages as a serial killer?"

"I'm a little bothered that you put the clothes on while thinking those things might be possibilities." He tucked his wallet into his pocket and grabbed his keys from the hook. Everything was exactly where he left it the night before. Just like always.

"In my defense"—she grinned widely—"this is really soft cotton." She ran her hand over the sleeve of the shirt and shrugged. "Whoever your murder victims were, they had wonderful taste."

"Those are my sister's things. She left them behind when she moved to Portland. I talked to her yesterday morning, and she was alive and well."

"Maybe she wouldn't want me wearing her stuff. She could want it back." The humor left Elaine's eyes and worry returned.

"Those were the clothes she wore four babies ago. I'm pretty sure when I offered to send them to her she told me to burn anything under a size six. You're welcome to whatever's in there."

"I won't need much else past today. I have a plan. A thirty-day plan." She seemed to have calmed a bit, finding out she wasn't wearing the cast-off clothes of dead people.

"Thirty days?" He snickered. "I can't figure out if you're spontaneous or a planner."

"Usually I plan," she replied brightly, looking ready to give a presentation. "I've had a ten-year plan since I was ten years old. I'm taking a break from that. I did a lot of logistical thinking this morning. Realistically my bank is not going to send me new credit cards if I can't prove I am who I am, or where I am. My purse is locked up in my office at work in New York."

"Why not have someone ship it to you?" Davis asked, still trying to piece everything together. What makes a woman like this run away with nothing and no plan?

"I'd prefer not to do that. And I don't need to. All

I need is enough money to eat and pay for a place to live for the next thirty days. I'll get a job that can guarantee that. If you can agree to a few terms."

"Terms?" Davis asked, scanning her face as if she might break out into a laugh any moment. But she never faltered. She might as well be a bank employee explaining a transaction to him at this point.

"Yes. It's a lot to ask, but I need you to make a hundred-dollar investment in my plan. In two weeks I can pay you back with interest. Also could you reach out to Dallas and see if he'd be willing to let me stay in a cabin for a week or so before I can pay him?" Her face was tight with seriousness, and he felt bad for the smirk he couldn't hold in.

"An investment? I think I can manage that. I'm sure Dallas would be happy to put you up in one of his older cabins. It's nothing fancy,"

"That's fine," she said, cutting him off. "I don't need much. This is a reset. I'm just taking the next thirty days to get myself straight."

"That's good," Davis nodded, still fighting the urge to laugh. "Mrs. Donavan needs help at her floral shop. Her daughter left for college, and she's short-handed now. She has a wedding at the end of the week. I bet if I put in a good word for you, she'd ask you to work today."

"Perfect," Elaine sang happily as she spun her hair into a ponytail. "I could do well there."

"You have experience as a florist?" he asked, continuing to knock on the truth door and hoping she accidently opened it.

"I have seen flowers before," she edged out,

finally breaking into a grin herself. "But I'm a quick learner. See everything is coming together."

"Help yourself to more of the clothes in there." He pulled out his wallet from his back pocket and fished out some cash. "Here's my investment in your reboot."

"Reset," she corrected, taking the money and tucking it into her pocket. "That's exactly what I need."

"Because of what happened," he said causally, tiding up a few things on the counter.

"Nice try," she replied pointing a scolding finger at him. "There's nothing there to talk about. I do want to thank you for all you've done, but now I'm ready to get back to being independent."

"Because depending on people is a bad thing?" he asked, adding another leading question to the pile.

"It's dangerous," she said, using her palms to press the invisible wrinkles out of her cotton shirt. "I prefer to take care of myself."

Davis nodded his agreement but couldn't help but add his two cents, "After I lent you some money and clothes, helped you find a place to stay, and found you a job?"

"Yes"—she chuckled—"but then that's it."

"Come on, I'll give you a ride to Mrs. Donavan's. Then I'll get your car fueled up and brought into town today," he said, pulling on his baseball hat.

"Then that's it," she said through her coy smile. "Then I'll be fine."

"Right," he sighed as he headed out the door.

"You will be fine, Elaine."

"And your investment will be worth it. I'll make sure this is all worth your while," she added, her cheeks growing a little pinker. His intention wasn't to make her feel bad. He had no problem helping her out. But he had to admit the blush in her cheeks only made her more attractive.

"It's not a problem," he said, turning on her suddenly and looking her square in the eyes. "I'm giving you a hard time. It's no trouble at all. Everyone needs a reset now and then. I can respect that."

"How about you?" she asked as he opened her door and she climbed into the passenger side of his truck. The only woman who'd been in that spot in the last four years was old Widow Marcelo, who'd needed to get her dogs to the vet in a hurry. Elaine looked lightyears better with the early morning light shining on her blonde hair. "Do you ever need a reset?" she pressed.

"Me?" he grunted, sliding into the driver's side. "No. I'm a simple guy. I wake up. Go to work. Eat. Tinker around on my own boat. Go to bed. Not much there that needs fixing."

"We'd have to agree to disagree on that. There's way more to life than just that. I find it hard to believe a man like you in a place like this doesn't have girls falling all over him. It must be a full time job trying to stay single."

"It's a burden, but I manage." He chuckled. "But you, there must be a man up in New York wondering where you went. Aren't you worried there'll be an all-points bulletin going out for you soon? I'm only asking because if you're in my truck when they find you, I don't want to go down for kidnapping."

"Trust me, you're safe. No one is wondering where I am. Which makes this little vacation perfect. I'm beholden to no one. Well, except you because I owe you a hundred dollars now."

"What happens after thirty days?" Davis asked, fixing his eyes on the road and trying not to look overly interested in her response.

"It doesn't work that way," she explained, as though this were some tried and true method of living. "I'll know in thirty days what I should do. I know it'll all work out fine. That little breakdown last night. That's not me. I can get through this."

"Well," he said, throwing her a sideways glance, "I certainly wouldn't bet against you."

Chapter Five

"You just need to clip all these stems down to about here," Mrs. Donavan explained as she used her calloused hands to push her thick glasses back into position. Her curly white hair rose from her head like springs and bounced as she moved around the tiny shop from flower to flower. "After that you can cut these ribbons in one foot lengths. Can you handle that?"

"Yes ma'am," Elaine nodded, ignoring her instinct to explain how painfully over qualified she was for this job. She'd spent the last ten years positioning herself as a key player, trading on the New York Stock Exchange. She'd clawed her way through every barrier and made a name for herself. Surely cutting the stems off some lilies was manageable. "I just want to let you know again how grateful I am that you hired me on such short notice."

"Any friend of Davis is a friend of mine," Mrs. Donavan said, smiling warmly at Elaine. "That boy has been good to me over the years. How exactly is it you know him again?"

"He helped me out when I found myself in a tough spot," Elaine explained, not wanting to lie to the kind woman.

"And is there anything special between you two?" Mrs. Donavan asked, her smile spreading wide and her watery gray blue eyes glimmering with excitement. "He can't possible continue the lifestyle he has."

"What lifestyle is that?" Elaine asked, measuring with impeccable precision as she cut the stems. If you were going to do something, it was best to do it perfectly.

"Oh he's been punishing himself for over four years. It's pathetic. When he walked in here with you I thought, finally he's moving on. Was I wrong?"

"Sorry to say I'm not his love interest," Elaine apologized, her cheeks warm with embarrassment. "We've done more yelling at each other since we've met than anything else. He's just a good guy helping out. What exactly is he punishing himself for?"

"Don't you know?" Mrs. Donavan asked, arranging and rearranging a few vases and eyeing Elaine skeptically. "Surely someone told you."

"No," Elaine said, shaking her head and snipping the last few lilies. "I tried not to pry."

"I'm not gonna spill his secrets all over these flowers," Mrs. Donavan said, feigning righteous indignation. "But I will tell you it's far past time for him to move on. That girl was not his responsibility. Her mistakes. Her choices. That boy has just been beating himself up all this time. It's high time he let all that go."

"Seems like an interesting story," Elaine said, trying to imagine what kind of situation Davis and his big heart might have gotten into years ago.

"He had a high school sweetheart," Mrs. Donavan explained in a whisper as though the volume made it less scandalous. “Julie Brown-Styles.” She shook her head in disappointment. “Prom queen to his prom king. Cheerleader to his star quarterback. We all thought they’d be married and having kids in no time.”

“Sounds like they were meant to be,” Elaine commented, surprised to hear that aloof Davis was ever the center of attention. She couldn’t picture him dancing in some school gymnasium with a plastic crown on his head, reigning over prom.

“On paper,” Mrs. Donavan agreed. “But she had her sights set on California for years. Somewhere along the way she decided she was going to be an actress. They were together a couple years after high school, and then she acted like this town and his love was suffocating her. It was supposed to only be a year out there. But she came back with a piercing in her nose, a stranger on her arm, and a penchant for alcoholic beverages. It broke him. Not only because he thought they had a future, but because he also saw how she’d changed. She was the shell of the woman she once was. That place wrecked her, and he felt like it was his fault for not giving her more reasons to stay in Indigo Bay. He was sure if he’d have loved her harder or begged her more he could have kept her safe. But you and I, and everyone else in this town, knows you can’t tie a donkey to a tree and think he’s gonna be happy forever.”

“Right,” Elaine said tentatively as she tried to process the metaphor. “You can’t love someone into doing what’s best for them. If you could there’d be a lot less trouble in the world.”

"Isn't that the truth?" Mrs. Donavan remarked, patting her shoulder as if they'd been friends for years. "The problem was every once in a while when she was down on her luck she'd come back a mess, and he'd clean her up while she strung him along. Then like always, she'd leave again."

Elaine arranged the flowers and nodded intently. "She sounds like a real heartbreaker. Should I be on the lookout for her pulling in? Let me guess, she drives a little red corvette?"

"Close," Mrs. Donavan replied solemnly, and Elaine realized instantly she'd made a mistake. "It was a cherry red convertible she drove off the side of a cliff in California. No one knows for sure if it was an accident or if she was just giving up. I suspect too many drinks that night. She and Davis had just had one of their epic breakups. Right in the middle of town square he told her to go and never come back. He was finally done with her."

"Ouch," Elaine said, knowing she sounded like an idiot, but at a loss for more poetic words. "That's so sad. No wonder he hasn't dated anyone since."

"It was a waste of a good man and just one more way she ruined him even after she was gone." She did the sign of the cross and whispered a quick prayer. "Not to speak ill of the dead, but he's better off without her. I just hope he can bounce back one of these days. A nice girl needs to come along and snap him out of it." A silence fell between them until Mrs. Donavan began to hum and throw her sideways glances.

"Don't look at me like that," Elaine said, quickly

dropping the flowers out of her hands. "I'm the absolute worst thing that could happen to him right now. Like I said when you hired me, I'm only here for a month. I'd be just another woman running out of his life."

"But you think he's attractive?" Mrs. Donavan asked, humming while she waited for an answer.

"He's not my type," Elaine dodged, but she had a feeling Mrs. Donavan was skilled in this particular type of interrogation. The kind that got to the bottom of people's feelings. "He's a little rugged for me. I'm from New York. I tend to date business professionals."

"Davis is no slouch. He owns his own repair business, and you didn't answer my question. Don't you find him attractive?"

"I do," Elaine answered, her cheeks flushing pink as the words spilled out. "But I am honestly only staying here a month at most. It wouldn't be fair to him."

"I'm not suggesting you get married," Mrs. Donavan explained, circling around the wide table to grab some roses. "I'm just saying maybe you could help blow the stink off him. Don't you think?"

"I'm not familiar enough with that expression to agree." Elaine laughed, shaking her head at the turn this conversation had taken. "But please don't explain it to me." They both broke into a laugh as they began arranging the flowers.

"There's a certain way to make sure your bouquets come out just right," Mrs. Donavan explained, the skin around her eyes wrinkled as she scrutinized the first arrangement. "People always think it has to be balanced. Equal amounts of every flower, nothing out of place. But that's not true. A good bouquet is beautiful when you take risks. You can't always be looking for symmetry and perfection. Sometimes you just have to toss in what feels right and trust your heart."

"Are we still talking about roses?" Elaine asked, with a devilish grin.

"Just clip those stems, girl," Mrs. Donavan sighed, winking as she headed to the back room. "Take some risks."

Chapter Six

"Hi there, Mrs. Donavan," Davis said, nodding his hello to the hunched-shouldered older woman he'd known since he was born. She was one of the hardest working women in town and he respected how seriously she took her responsibilities. By day a florist. By night a meddler in all matters of the heart.

"Davis," she sang back lovingly. "What an exquisite girl you brought to me. She has a real knack for arranging flowers."

"Really?" Davis asked as Elaine came around the corner.

"Please don't look so surprised." Elaine smirked as she folded her apron and laid it over the back of the chair. "Thank you for all lessons you gave me today, Mrs. Donavan. I learned so much."

"Only one lesson that matters." She grinned, her coiled white hair bouncing as she walked. "Don't forget. Risks, darling. That's what makes a beautiful bouquet."

"Yes ma'am," Elaine said, accepting the warm hug Mrs. Donavan was offering. "I'll be back tomorrow. Davis has my car squared away so I'll be here bright and early."

"What a lovely thing to do," Mrs. Donavan said, pulling Davis in for a hug as well. "Two lovely young people in such close proximity to each other, how nice. But don't rush in here tomorrow. Maybe you two should stop at Sweet Caroline's and have some breakfast."

"Yes," Davis said, rushing Elaine toward the door. The bell chimed overhead and they were out on the curb and under the warm sun before Elaine could reply.

"You're in a hurry," Elaine said, looking him over as he dashed to open the passenger door in his truck.

"Mrs. Donavan has a nasty habit of talking your ear off if you stick around too long. Plus she's one of the big matchmakers in Indigo Bay. She, Mrs. Caroline, and Lucille spend most of their free time trying to work out everyone's life for them."

"She was charming," Elaine said, her wide smile lighting her face. She looked even more beautiful after a day's work than she had when she left this morning. He fought to stay focused on anything else. "Though I do think you're right. Mrs. Donavan seemed hell-bent on fixing you up."

"I suppose she told you all about Julie?" Davis asked, hardly needing Elaine to answer. Her cheeks grew pink and her lips smacked shut abruptly; that was all the answer he needed. "It's fine. I knew the minute I dropped you off there this morning she'd be blabbing all my business. If it wasn't her, it would be someone else. People around here, they don't know what boundaries are. It doesn't bother me."

"I'm sorry anyway," Elaine offered, looking sheepish now. "It sounds like you really loved her, and it took its toll on you."

"Believe it or not"—he sighed—"I'm in a much better place than most people give me credit for. I don't cry myself to sleep. I don't beat myself up." He put the truck in reverse and pulled onto the main street.

"But you don't date anyone either? That's a long time to be alone." She shifted in her seat and stared out the window as if there were something interesting to see.

"Just because I don't go parading my love life up and down Indigo Bay doesn't mean I don't have one. When I was with Julie, we were the focal point here. Everything we did was public information. Our good days, our bad days, everyone knew what we were doing and when. I swore I'd never do that again. Let them talk. Let them wonder. I just don't give them anything to talk about anymore."

"It must be nice to know people care though," she tried in a cheery voice. "In New York everyone is in their own bubble. We walk fast, we talk fast, and we rarely look up long enough to notice if anyone needs anything. I'm going to enjoy the next thirty days here, soaking in all the kindness."

"You'll need a place to stay then," Davis said, happy to start talking about something other than his past. "I talked to Dallas. He has one small cabin he said you'd be welcomed to use. It's on the back of the property, and he said he hasn't been out there much lately. I told him I'd check it out with you and make sure it'll work. Your car is fueled and at my house. I'll get it over to the cabin for you later."

"Thank you," she said, looking guilty. "I hate

that you've had to do so much to help me. I promise I'll get Dallas his rent money for the cabin, and I'll pay you back for everything."

"I'm sure you will," Davis nodded. "I'm in no rush. Do what you need to do to feel better. Then I'm sure when you get back to New York, it'll be nice."

"I'm never going back to New York," she scoffed, shaking her head defiantly. "I might not know much about where I'm going to end up, but it certainly isn't there."

"Really?" Davis asked. "I wouldn't think you could just leave a fast-paced lifestyle without looking back. What about your job?"

"My job is gone," she admitted, unrolling her window and putting her arm out, letting the wind blow through her fingers. "And I won't be able to find something in my field again. That ship has sailed."

"What field was that?" he asked casually, as though he was trying to keep a skittish deer from running off.

"Plus"—she had no intention of answering him—"I actually enjoyed working around all those flowers this morning. Maybe that will be my new profession."

"Hold on," Davis said, as he cut the wheel and pulled onto the dirt trail leading to the cabin Dallas had offered Elaine. "It's a little bumpy. When you drive your car here you'll have to go real slow. Those sports cars aren't built for this kind of road."

"Is this a road?" she asked, clutching the handle over her head as they bounced over another rough spot.

"Yeah, this is more secluded than I thought it would be. I haven't been down this side of the property since I was a kid. We used to come out here and light barn fires and drink. I know if Dallas had anything else available he'd give it to you."

"It'll be fine," she said, but her face looked less convinced. "I can make do anywhere. I'm not some pretentious northerner who can't take care of herself. I've been doing it long enough."

"It should be just around this bend," Davis said, trying to navigate around a tree limb that had fallen.

"Please tell me that's not it." Elaine sighed, rising in her seat to get a better look. "Because I can make do with a lot, but I will need a roof."

"Oh man," Davis grunted as he pulled in. "We had a bad wind storm here a couple weeks ago. That tree must have come down then." He hopped out of the truck and hurried over to the cabin. "Dallas is gonna have to send a crew out here to repair that roof. It might take a few days."

She was out of the truck and by his side a moment later. "I mean it's not that bad. Maybe if I only stay on that side of the cabin?"

"Sure," he chuckled as long as you don't mind the animals that have probably moved in by now. I'm sure the raccoons make for good company in the middle of the night."

"He doesn't have any other cabins at all?" she asked, nibbling her nails nervously. "I mean even something being renovated, I could stay out of the way."

"I'll call him again," Davis said, walking over to the fallen tree and trying to figure out what Dallas would need to get it fixed up. "Worst case you can come back to my place."

"I've asked enough of you already," she said, shaking her head and kicking at the dirt with the sneakers she'd borrowed from his sister. "Not to mention how much fuel we'd add to the gossip mill."

"I'm not worried about that," he said, waving her off. "They'll talk no matter what. But it's definitely not suitable for you to be here, and it may be days before Dallas can get anything else open. We can head to town and get some groceries. I should make you a proper dinner."

"You cook?" she asked, propping her hands high on her hips as though he'd been holding out on her. "I'd like to see that."

"I have a few recipes I can manage. Nothing like you ate at Sweet Caroline's last night. There won't be cobbler, but it's stick to the ribs kind of food. When I went in to see Caroline this morning she said you were much too thin and to make sure I work on that."

"I'm starting to really like this place," Elaine said, hopping back into his truck. "But are you sure you don't mind putting me up for a few days?"

"It'll be nice to have the company," he admitted, taking his time to back up the truck and turn it around in such a tight spot. "The house is pretty quiet."

"I feel like I owe you something," she sputtered out, twisting her chin up thoughtfully.

"No," he cut back quickly. "I don't want you feeling like that. Just enjoy your time in Indigo Bay.

Think of me as an ambassador, a welcoming committee. I'm doing my obligatory small-town duty."

"How about a little honesty," she offered, fidgeting in her seat. "I guess the least I can do is tell you more about myself."

"That would be nice, considering Mrs. Donavan gave you my whole life story. You could even the score a little."

"I'm a VP at a large trading firm on Wall Street," Elaine breathed out reluctantly. "Or I was. I grew up in the city, and all I ever wanted to do was stand on the floor of the New York Stock exchange and trade. It didn't pan out exactly how I thought it would. I didn't have the right makeup for it. So I went on the equities research side instead."

"Wow, a VP sounds like you've earned your stripes," Dallas replied, watching her try to hide her pride about it all.

"It's a long process. Right out of college I went in as essentially an unpaid intern. Then I did some syndicate desk work, issuing bonds. I went to Harvard business school for two years and came back as an analyst. I've been working my way up. It's a very intense job."

"I'm embarrassed to say I don't know much about that. I mean I've seen it on television, but it always looked like a bunch of people waving papers around and yelling."

"As far as the trading floor, that's pretty much it." She laughed, and he felt relieved to see her relaxed enough to talk about herself. "You make trades auction style on behalf of your clients until the closing bell. It's fast-paced. There are billions of dollars on the line. My role was to research and essentially grade pending IPOs and other opportunities on the horizon." Her hands fluttered with excitement as she spoke. "The stakes are so high. And I was good. They used to call me a bloodhound for a money-making opportunity. I made our firm a fortune."

"That sounds a lot like the livestock auctions my uncle took me to when I was young and visited his farm," Davis teased, and she rolled her eyes.

"Sure if each cow was worth a million dollars and you had to know how they'd perform compared to the cow next to them."

"If you were so good at it, why stop? Why would you want to leave New York if you loved it so much? It's your home." Dallas knew he was edging on thin ice and was one intrusive question away from plunging into freezing water.

"You've been here your whole life?" she asked, casting a knowing look at him, hardly needing to finish her point but doing it anyway. "Indigo Bay is all you've known, and you love it? Or are you just comfortable here? Complacent?"

"A little of that I guess." He shrugged. "I had the opportunity to go other places over the years, and it never worked out."

"California?" Elaine asked, arching her brow at him.

"Yes," he sighed. "I could have gone with Julie. My sister was here though. She's two years younger, and she didn't want to move away with my parents either. I told them I'd stay with her. It's a commitment I'm glad I made because it worked out well for her. She's very happy now. But I do wonder about Julie. If I had gone with her maybe she wouldn't have spiraled the way she did."

"My mother was always good at giving advice. She used to say don't take all the credit for other people's mistakes. You'd be amazed how little control you have over helping someone do the right thing." She touched his forearm gently, and he kept his eyes fixed on the road as they emerged from the woods and onto the main road.

"Maybe so," he reluctantly agreed. "What's done is done. But to answer your question, I'm happy in Indigo Bay. It's not because I don't know any better."

"I'm not as enlightened as you, maybe. I thought I loved New York, but the second I started driving away from it, the city lights in my rearview mirror, I felt a weight lift off me. Landing in a place like this makes me think maybe there is more to life than just waking up every morning, trying to make a bunch of strangers a lot of money."

"You managed to not answer any of my questions," he said, throwing her a sideways glance but making sure to flash her a smile too. "You didn't say why you left your job."

"And I probably won't ever tell you," she shot back defiantly. "It's not a high point of my life. You saw how desperate I was to leave it behind. We met on a curb; that should tell you all you need to know."

"Fair enough," Davis conceded. "Know that

Indigo Bay is happy to have you. You're welcome here as long as you like."

"Thanks." She grinned. "How did you get to be such a nice guy? It must be exhausting always running in and saving the day for a damsel in distress."

"You are a full time job so far," he joked but then fell serious. "Actually, I don't think you're a damsel in distress at all, Elaine. I don't think you need a knight to come slay your dragon; all you need is a sword of your own. I'm happy to help with that."

"Damn," she said, her hand covering her face as she leaned out the window, her hair blowing wildly.

"What?" he asked, wondering if he'd done something wrong.

"You're good, Davis Mills." She laughed loudly, though it was eaten up by the wind. "You are one of the very good ones."

Chapter Seven

"I can practically hear the gears of the rumor mill being greased right now," Elaine said quietly as she leaned into Davis's broad shoulder. "The two of us food shopping together. Scandalous."

"You don't know the half of it," he whispered back. "That woman who practically ran up the dairy aisle in her high heels was Lucille. She's the town busybody, and I guarantee she left her shopping cart where it was and started hitting speed dial to spread the news. She'll have our wedding planned by the end of the week."

"That doesn't bother you?" Elaine asked, scanning the frozen food section for something that looked remotely like one of the diet meals she normally heated up at the end of the long day.

"They've had me linked to much less attractive women before. You're far from the worst person I've been fake engaged to."

"That's a glowing review," she teased. "Where is all the healthy food?" she asked, finally starting to open the doors to the frozen food and move things around.

"What are you talking about? All this food is locally sourced, grown within a hundred miles. Most organic. You can't get better than this. What are you looking for?"

"I like these frozen meals that are like three hundred calories. There's a broccoli one I usually get, but I don't see anything like that."

"And you won't," he assured her with a high and mighty grin. "That's not a real meal. It's just chemicals molded into the shape of food. You can't actually enjoy those."

"I don't," she admitted, rolling her eyes. "But I do enjoy not having to buy bigger clothes every month. I enjoy not having to turn the oven on when I get home at ten at night. My job"—she hesitated remembering how her life had changed—"my old job had me out all hours of the day and night. I could have grabbed takeout and greasy food like most of the guys, but I probably wouldn't have had a job much longer."

"Why not?" Davis asked, stopping the cart abruptly and twisting his face up, seeming to know the answer already. "You had to be skinny to work there?"

"An unwritten rule at my particular firm. You're working with clients every day, you're the face of the firm. There is a certain expectation. I consider myself a feminist. It insulted the heck out of me, but some games have rules, and if you want to win, you play by them."

"That's ridiculous; some of the best women I've known in my life were curvy. Some were short, some wore overalls. Any boss that makes you count your calories is an idiot."

"That we can agree on. My boss was an idiot. But it doesn't matter now because I don't work there anymore. The only thing that matters now is what kind of flowers Mrs. Donavan wants me to trim. I'll tie whatever ribbon she needs into bows. Maybe she'll keep me so busy I won't be able to run in the mornings anymore. Which means I'd still like to get some of those low calorie meals."

"Maybe stop counting your calories and start counting your blessings," a nasally voice called from over her shoulder.

"Lucille," Davis laughed as he flashed a warm smile. "I thought I saw you in the dairy aisle. How are you?"

"Who cares how I'm doing?" she replied quickly, waving him off and keeping her eyes fixed possessively on Elaine. "How are you two doing? What are you two doing? Why are you doing it?"

"That's a lot of questions, Lucille," Davis said, grabbing some more items off the shelf and hardly sparing the old nosy woman the one thing she was craving. Attention. "This is Elaine. She's new in town. I'm guessing you've heard about her from Caroline by now. Or maybe Mrs. Donavan. You have no shortage of operatives here in Indigo Bay."

"Hmm," Lucille said, as if he were holding back the good stuff. "Our network is very thorough. But we're always looking for the latest updates. Straight from the horse's mouth if we can get it."

"I don't hear anyone neighing over here," Davis said, looking up and down the aisle sarcastically.

Lucille was not impressed. "I heard she rolled in during the middle of the night without a penny to her name and looking like a hot mess. But you swooped in and saved the day."

"Not exactly," Davis corrected, and Elaine stayed quiet. "But she will be coming to stay in my spare room for a few days. Dallas had a cabin for her but the last storm knocked a tree through the roof."

"How lucky," Lucille sang out, clapping her hands together in excitement.

"I'm guessing Dallas doesn't think so," Davis corrected, clearly loving this banter.

"Dallas's bad luck is your good fortune. But what brings you to the supermarket?"

"I'm picking up some nails and lumber," he teased. "I'm going to see if they have a carburetor for my old truck."

"You're going to make her dinner aren't you?" Lucille took an intrusive inventory of the items in his cart and nodded her approval.

"The girl's got to eat," Davis said matter-of-factly. "What kind of host would I be if I let her starve?"

"Right," Lucille sang, her high heels skittering a bit as she hustled to keep up with them. "And it looks like you're making your mom's meatloaf?"

"I am," Davis confirmed. "You think that's a good choice? She doesn't strike me as much of a down-home meatloaf kind of girl, but it's the recipe I know the best."

Elaine giggled as the two of them continued to talk as if she wasn't there. But she still didn't speak up.

Lucille thought it over, her face showing deep deliberation. "I think that would be fine. It's not particularly romantic. You can light some candles maybe to make up for that. Perhaps make a little salad too. Judging by her figure, or lack of it I should say, I bet she'll want something green too."

"What about dessert?" Elaine interrupted, elbowing her way into the conversation finally. "Do you plan to make anything, because if not I have a recipe that'll . . ." she hesitated as she thought on it. "Boy I need to borrow some southern sayings if I'm going stick around down here."

"The recipe will have you begging for mercy, and you'll be full as a boot," Lucille offered seriously. "You've got yourself some of the most beautiful hair I've ever seen. Davis have you seen her hair? It's like golden spun silk."

"Hmm," Davis said, eying Elaine with a bemused smile. "I hadn't notice she had hair before this, but now that you mention it, you're right. It's very pretty."

Lucille slapped his shoulder and grunted in frustration at the pain it caused her own hand. "What are you made of, rocks?"

"Just in my head," he replied seriously, knocking on his forehead.

Lucille turned toward Elaine, looking completely exasperated. "I hope you like a smart aleck because this boy is the worst. You'd think with a face like his and the way he fills out the back of those jeans he'd be dragged down the aisle by now, but no ring on that finger after all this time."

"It's a tragedy of epic proportions," Elaine said with feigned seriousness. "It's like having a prize winning pig and leaving him in the barn."

"Exactly," Lucille said, sounding relieved at the common ground they'd found. It seemed to hit her like a sudden ocean wave that she was the butt of their joke. "Oh, well," she huffed, "aren't you two the perfect pair? It's nice to finally see you've met a girl who can keep up with you." Her face was soft and forgiving as she patted his shoulder, and he leaned down to plant a kiss on her cheek.

"If only you'd give me a chance, Lucille." He sighed. "If you'd stop breaking my heart, maybe I could find love someday."

"Son," she scolded with a wrinkled finger wagging in his direction, "you and I both know I'm way out of your league."

"Goodnight, Lucille," he said as she scampered away to find her shopping cart. Turning back toward Elaine, he moaned, "Welcome to Indigo Bay, where your business is everyone's business."

"You're a good sport," he said, his eyes fixed on her face for a long beat. When the moment grew quiet between them, just long enough to be noticed by them both, he cleared his throat. "So you're making dessert. Should I be nervous? Is it gluten free, nut free, sugar free, flavor free?"

"You'll like it, trust me. If I can remember the recipe," she said, tapping her chin thoughtfully. "I'll go round up the ingredients and meet you at the front." She hurried away and prayed they'd have everything she needed. It had been ages since she made her grandmother's cream cheese pound cake, but she knew it was just the kind of thing Davis would love.

By the time she had all the ingredients balancing precariously in her arms, Davis was standing at the front of the store chatting with another group of older women.

"Oh and speak of the devil," one of the women cooed as she gestured for all the others to turn. "Her hair is beautiful. Lucille was right."

"Thank you," Elaine said, self-consciously rebalancing the groceries in one arm so she could push her hair back behind her ears. A couple things tumbled to the ground and bounced in every direction. "Oh I'm such a klutz," she said, scolding herself.

"Let me help," Davis insisted, first taking the remaining things from her arm and placing them down on the check-out belt. He quickly rounded up everything that fell and, with his hand on the small of her back, led her past the women gathered to see her.

"I feel like a gorilla at the zoo," she whispered. "Everyone is just lining up to see me."

"A gorilla with golden spun silk hair," he corrected. "Let's check out and get back to my place."

"Your groceries have been paid for," the pimply-faced kid behind the cash register announced as though he was reading it from a script.

"Who paid for our groceries?" Davis asked, eyeing the giggling women behind him. "That was completely unnecessary."

"The only message I'm supposed to give you is use the money you saved and take this girl on a proper date." The nervous boy began bagging the groceries as quickly as he could. His face was as red as a hot ember.

"That was so nice," Elaine said, loud enough for the women to hear her in case one of them had paid the bill. "What a lovely place Indigo Bay is. I'm so glad to be here."

"And we're glad to have you," a woman wearing a pastel polo shirt and stunning pearls chirped, and the others all nodded in agreement. "He's a bit of a pain but one of the finest men for miles. Don't let him scare you off."

Another woman, with one of the largest diamond rings Elaine had ever seen, stepped forward and chimed in, "The blustery front is just that. Ignore it. He's like a cactus on the outside but a teddy bear on the inside. Don't give up on him."

"I hear what you're saying," Elaine offered weakly. "It's just that I'm—"

"Come on, honey," Davis said, lacing his fingers in hers and tugging her away. "Let's go to my place."

They were out the front door, but the excited voices of strangers nipped at their heels.

"You are fueling the fire. They're going to be gossiping nonstop about that." Elaine giggled as she climbed into the passenger side of his truck. "I feel like we're on the run."

"Aren't you though?" he asked, as he put the truck in reverse and sped out of the grocery parking lot. "Now you've got me running with you."

Chapter Eight

"You look good in an apron," Davis teased. "The flour all over your cheeks doesn't hurt either." He reached a hand up and swiped gently at the white dust.

"I'm, admittedly, out of practice," she confessed with a smirk. "But I think you're going to love this recipe. I ate it all the time when I was little."

"I pictured you as a ten-year-old, heating up those sad little diet frozen meals. It's good to know at one point in your life food was your friend."

"Food was my friend until metabolism was my enemy," she explained, stirring the batter with all her might.

"The meatloaf will be ready in a little while. Then the oven is all yours. Do you like baked or mashed potatoes?"

"Potatoes," she sang, and he laughed at the euphoria filling her face. "I miss potatoes the most, really. Let's do real buttery mashed potatoes. Maybe add a little cheese?"

"I'm creating a monster," Davis joked as he rounded the small kitchen and grabbed what he needed from her left and her right. The smell of her skin filled his nose and made him linger close for a long moment.

"Are you inspecting my work?" she asked,

turning the batter so he could see it. "I don't remember hovering over your meatloaf."

"You're right." He tossed his hands up and backed away slowly. "So this was your grandmother's recipe?" he asked, never tiring of hearing her voice and learning what little fragments of history built her into the woman she was before they'd met.

"Yes. Estella Monroe Gladwell. The most ambitious women I've ever met. She was always lightyears before her time. She went to college. Got a job outside the house while raising a family."

"What did she do?" Davis asked, peeling the potatoes and chopping them up for the pot.

"She was a numbers wiz. Some kind of a savant. I don't know exactly what her title was, but she worked for an engineering company. I got the chance to go to work with her when I was very small, and I fell in love with the way people treated her. My mother was a stay-at-home mom. She supported my father and his career. There was always clean laundry for him. Always a warm plate of food when he came home. She was a good wife and a great mom, but it never felt like something I could understand. But Grandma Gladwell, I understood her. She's what made me work so hard."

"Your parents are in Europe, right?" Davis asked, impressing her with his memory of the rambling details she'd given. "Do you see them much?"

"I'm embarrassed to say I judged my father very harshly. I went a long time before seeing them at all.

It's a little better now, but at the time I was young and sitting through classes learning about ethics and business practices. I couldn't understand how someone could get themselves in that kind of trouble. Just do the right thing. It sounded so simple at the time. Now I see how quickly you can fall and how easy it can be to run." Elaine stopped stirring the batter suddenly, and her gaze was fixed on an empty spot on the wall.

Davis rinsed his hands and patted them dry on a towel before walking over to her. "You aren't your father, and you aren't your grandmother. You are you, and one moment in time doesn't define your life. Trust me, if it did, I'd never leave the house."

"You hardly do," she teased, beating back the sadness and returning to him. "Work doesn't count. Look, even tonight we're in here cooking."

"I'm supposed to put the grocery money aside and take you on a proper date. That'll show you I'm not some sad recluse who spends all my time hiding from the world."

"What kind of dates do people go on in Indigo Bay?" Elaine asked, back at the project at hand, pouring the batter into the pan.

"You'll have to wait and see. I'm guessing it'll be different than any date you've been on in the city, that's for sure."

The oven beeped, indicating his meatloaf was done. He opened the oven and took the meatloaf out, bobbling it when the dish towel proved too thin for the heat stinging his fingers.

"Watch it," Elaine said, as the slow motion

juggling act came to an end with the meatloaf pan landing upside down on the floor by their feet. "Are you burned?" Elaine asked, taking his nicked up, callous-covered hands in hers and inspecting them closely.

"The only damage is to my pride," he groaned, shaking his head in frustration. "I don't have a backup plan for dinner besides an enormous bowl of mashed potatoes."

"Followed by cream cheese pound cake. As long as you don't juggle that I think we'll be fine. It's not really about the food anyway," she assured him, gently rubbing his shoulder. "It's just nice to be here. Talking. Forgetting everything else out there." She gestured out the door as though that's where the monsters and trouble lurked.

"One of these days you'll tell me what you're hiding from, won't you?" Davis asked, tucking some loose hair behind her ears. He tilted her chin upward so her eyes couldn't dart to the floor. "Not right now. But someday?"

"I will," she acquiesced, sucking her bottom lip in and nibbling it nervously. The space between them was shrinking, though he wasn't sure if it was him leaning in or her. He just knew their lips were getting closer, and the desire to kiss her was at a boiling point.

"I'm sorry about the meatloaf," he whispered. "I'll make it up to you." They were just a breath apart, and she nodded a tiny, nearly imperceptible nod that he took as an agreement to how exactly he could make up for the meatloaf.

When their lips finally touched Davis felt as though they'd been welded together. Not just the way his fingers spun up in her hair or the way hers clutched at his shirt. It was deeper than the surface. The kiss was perfect; the connection was deep.

The oven chirped again, Davis having forgotten to cancel out the timer. The noise was enough to bring them back to the moment. He pulled away reluctantly, his hand sliding down to her cheek and lingering there. "Mashed potatoes?" he asked, a devilish grin sliding across his face.

"And cake."

Chapter Nine

"A dance?" Elaine asked as Davis pulled his truck into a dirt parking lot loaded with other cars.

"It's a little fundraiser the Ashland Belle Society puts on every year. The society is made up of most of the nosy ladies you met at the grocery store. For all the trouble they stir up, they also provide a lot of help to people in need. It's why I don't mind cutting them some slack. They've been trying to get me to come to this event for a few years running, and I usually just volunteer for clean-up duty. This year I finally have a partner I don't mind being stuck next to for twelve hours."

"Twelve hours?" Elaine asked, eyeing the outdoor dance floor that had sparkling lights strung above it.

"It's a dance-a-thon," he explained, hopping out of the truck and rounding the front to open her door. She hesitated to step out.

"This proper date you've decided to take me on is a contest made up of dancing for hours on end?"

"To raise money for a good cause," he reminded her, his hand hanging there waiting for her to take it. "I figured you were the competitive type. And you're about forty years younger than half the contestants out there. Are you going to chicken out on me?"

"No," she answered instinctively. Elaine was

always a sucker for a dare, unable to turn down a challenge. Unlike most of her endeavors, however, this was a pretty intimate encounter. "I'm not chickening out. Is this really how you want to spend your night?"

"I can't think of anything I'd like better," he said, looking thoroughly relieved when she finally stepped out. "It'll be fun, I promise. The Ashland Belle Society knows how to have a good time."

"Davis," Caroline called, waving them over to the dance floor. It was lined on either side with white tents, filled with tables of food that Caroline seemed to be arranging. "I can't believe you actually came. This is going to be so much fun. Wait until the ladies see you."

"I figured we'd be the talk of the town tonight," Davis grinned, leaning down and planting a kiss on Caroline's cheek. "I ambushed Elaine though. She didn't know we were coming until just now."

"Ambush is the right word," Elaine groaned. "I'm not much of a dancer."

"Oh, you don't have to be," Caroline said, waving off her worry. "This is just for fun. Come over this way and get your tags. Lucille, look who's here."

"Well pluck the stars from the sky and call them diamonds," Lucille said, clutching her pearls and pretending to faint. "I can't believe we have these love birds as contestants tonight. The pledges will go through the roof for you two. Here are your numbers, just stick them to your shirts."

"Thank you," Elaine said, following the

instructions and secretly sizing up the competition. Davis was not wrong. Elaine liked to win. She liked to prove she was the best. It wasn't always the best quality but she reminded herself this was all for a good cause.

"Now, you get five minute breaks every hour to get a drink or something to eat and use the bathroom. Or," she whispered coyly, "to run off and kiss in private."

"I doubt anything we do tonight will be private," Davis countered. "But it's all for charity, right?"

"Right," Lucille agreed. "You can see the pledges here. Most of Indigo Bay will be here tonight. They'll come by and make pledge donations for every hour you dance." Lucille was positively glowing with excitement as she waltzed them around the area for a tour. "Caroline was sweet enough to provide the refreshments, and the music will be quite the assortment thanks to Mr. Nylie and his new downloading music device thingy. He's promised a wide variety of styles. That should keep you busy."

"What's the grand prize this year?" Davis asked, playfully nudging Elaine. "I'm feeling good about our odds."

"Don't underestimate your competition. They may be old, but they came to win. That's a very coveted prize you're dancing for."

"A new car?" Davis asked, goading her on.

"No, well not exactly. It is a form of transportation," Lucille explained, and Elaine could see there was something she was holding back. "It's an electric scooter meant for the retired community," she half mumbled. "Maybe not glamorous for you two but our normal contestants have someone in their lives who could benefit greatly from the prize. It even has all terrain tires so they can go down to the beach."

"Does it have a basket on the front?" Davis asked, looking very serious about the matter. "A bell?"

"It has a horn," Lucille corrected, pointing a threatening finger at him. "And it's too late to withdraw now. Your names are already on the board." She pointed over to a large white board off the side of the dance floor where a woman was hastily adding information. She'd just added *Davis Mills and Pretty Blonde.*

"Her name's Elaine," Davis said, pointing up at the board and frowning.

"I've been called worse," Elaine shrugged. "When does the dancing start?" Just as she finished speaking the music crackled to life on the speakers.

"Right now." Lucille grinned, pushing them out on to the dance floor. "All right contestants, it's time to get started. Let's see those dance moves."

A gaggle of mostly elderly people flooded the dance floor and coupled up. The first song was an old slow one that everyone cooed nostalgically about. Davis pulled her into his arms and spun her whimsically around the floor. "I hope you can keep up," he challenged with a breathy whisper in her ear.

"I hope so too," she laughed, giving herself over to him as he led her through the dance. "You're a better dancer than I would have thought."

"Lessons when I was a kid," he admitted

sheepishly. "My dad thought it would help me on the football field, and he was right. My footwork improved a ton. Once I got over the idea of wearing tights it wasn't so bad."

"Tights?" she asked, pulling away to see his face. "I can totally see you in tights."

"Enjoy that image because those days are over. At least you benefit from the torture I endured."

"So what are we going to talk about for the next twelve hours?" Elaine asked, starry-eyed and mesmerized by the twinkling overhead lights.

"We can dream up ways to use our new motorized scooter. Did you hear we can drive it on the beach?" He winked and Elaine practically felt her heart flutter.

"You are the best distraction I've ever had in my life," she said, resting her head on his chest. "You're funny, smart, and sweet. I'm so glad it was you who found me on that stupid curb."

"And that I didn't call the funny farm to have them come take you away. I'm happy to be your distraction. I hope it doesn't end at that though." The song shifted to a love ballad, and he swayed her back and forth to the slow beautiful beat.

"How long have you had the cabin?" Elaine asked, resting her head gently on his shoulder. "You don't strike me as a guy who wakes up and says, I want to live in a bright purple cabin."

"It wasn't purple when I bought it," Davis admitted. "Julie had been gone almost eight months, and I got wind that things weren't going great for her. There were rumors she might come back to Indigo

Bay. I had given her all the space I could, and it was killing me. I bought the cabin and painted it her favorite color. I fixed it up inside the way I knew she'd like it. I made it a home, hoping that when she saw it she could picture the rest of her life there with me. I spent months working on every detail."

"It didn't work?" Elaine asked, oozing with empathy. "She didn't stay."

"She did for a little while," Davis replied, attempting to sound upbeat. "But it wasn't real. None of it was. There was a big explosive fight about me trying to hold her back. She took off again."

"I'm sorry," Elaine offered, squeezing him a little tighter.

"Two hundred dollars on Davis and the pretty blonde," a voice called from one of the tents and every head turned. Davis was relieved something would break them out of this moment.

"Dallas," Davis groaned. "I figured you'd come watch the show."

"I was hoping you'd be back in your tights," Dallas joked, waving two hundred-dollar bills in the air. "If it's not too late to get them on, I'll double this donation."

"I like the sound of that," Elaine joked. "If I didn't already owe you a hundred dollars I'd go in on that donation myself."

"You don't owe me a thing, Elaine," Davis assured her, the smile leaving his face. "I mean it. Whatever you decide to do, I don't want you to feel any pressure from me. I really like that you're here. I'm glad you're feeling good right now. Life's all—"

"It's all mashed potatoes and cake," she smiled, remembering how something that had gone wrong could turn out just fine if you let it.

"Yes," he agreed, leaning down and kissing her cheek. "And I'm still hungry for more."

Chapter Ten

"I expected to see you pulling up on your new motorized scooter," Dallas called out to Davis as he loaded some lumber into his truck.

"We donated it to the Belle Society so they could do with it what they see fit," Davis corrected. "I hope I'm many years off from needing one of those."

"How many hours did you guys dance last night?" Dallas asked, gesturing for Davis to help while they talked. "That whole pile of wood needs to get in the bed of this truck."

"I came to thank you for the two-hundred-dollar donation and see how the cabin repair was going, not help you load wood. And we danced for six hours. That's about two hours longer than everyone else."

"Seemed like she was hard to let go of," Dallas said, tossing Davis a pair of work gloves from his pocket.

"She was and is," Davis admitted. "But she's a runner. I don't think Indigo Bay is big enough for a woman like that. Coming from New York City, I know she's running from something, but it'll eventually work itself out. When she doesn't need a place to hide anymore, I doubt she'll stay here."

"No word on what had her running in the first place? Don't you find it weird that she hasn't told you why she got in her car without her cell phone or purse and just started driving south?"

"She's a tough nut to crack," Davis sighed. "I'm trying not to push it. She'll tell me when she's ready, I'm sure."

"I can send my crew over to that cabin today if you want. They can probably have it patched and cleaned by tonight." Dallas stacked the wood up in the back of the truck and searched around for the straps to tie it down.

"No," Davis said, too quickly to sound natural. "I mean, you don't have to rush over there on my account. Things are all right where she is. I have space in the house. Plus she already has a recipe she wants to cook tonight. I'd hate to mess up her plans."

"Right," Dallas said, looking wholly unconvinced. "I'll give my crew something else to do this week and send them over next week."

"Sure," Davis agreed. "That'll work out well. You doing anything tonight?"

"I'm stopping by the café to help my mom work on one of the stoves that's acting up. Then I'm free."

"Why don't you come by for dinner," Davis croaked out awkwardly. "You haven't been to my place to eat in a while."

"I've never been to your house for dinner," Dallas corrected with a laugh. "I don't think you've been to your house for dinner either."

"I'm trying to change that. Elaine is something else. I really like her, and I'm hoping the more she gets to know people around here, the more she'll think about Indigo Bay as the place she could settle down. So come by at six, and see if your mom wants to join us."

"All right," Dallas said, skeptically. "I hope you know what you're doing with this girl. Aren't there any women in Indigo Bay you could go out with? I know Lucille has a list a mile long of local prospects. I don't want to see you getting torn up again if she leaves."

"If she leaves, she leaves," Davis lied as he helped tighten the strap over the lumber. "But I'm gonna give her some reasons to stay."

"If dinner with me is your big plan, I'm not feeling very confident for you."

"It's just one piece of it," Davis corrected. "I'm going to take her to all the best places in town."

"So that'll take about an hour, then what?"

"You know damn well this place is something special. I don't see you pulling up stakes and trying to leave. Indigo Bay has a little bit of magic in it. I just have to make sure she sees it."

Dallas hummed thoughtfully. "Take her to the old lighthouse," he offered. "I've got a telescope you can borrow. There's going to be a meteor shower tomorrow night. If the skies are clear, it'll be quite the show. It's roped off though, so you'll be breaking and entering."

"Exciting," Davis said, rolling his eyes. "If the cops come by, we'll make a run for it."

"Do you ever think of going to New York?" Dallas asked, swinging the door to his truck open but hesitating before getting in. "There's a big world outside of this place. If your plan fails, don't act like there's nothing else you could do."

"Do you need help unloading this on the other end?" Davis asked, clearing his throat uncomfortably. "I have another hour before I have to meet a client down by the pier to work on his boat."

"Sure," Dallas agreed gratefully. "We can swing by my cabin and grab the telescope."

"I didn't realize you were into astronomy," Davis laughed, hopping in the passenger seat of the truck.

"I bought it for the cabins. It's a nice feature for renters." He put the truck in gear and backed out quickly. "And maybe a little bit as a plan to impress the ladies."

"A failed plan?" Davis asked, looking worried.

"Yep, but it wasn't the telescope that failed me. Just point that thing at the sky tomorrow night, and if you really think Indigo Bay is the magic you need, it'll work."

"Try to look presentable for dinner tonight," Davis cut in. "Maybe ditch the sweaty shirt and dirty boots before you come over."

"You don't want me looking too good," Dallas said, kicking up some dirt as they headed out onto the main road. "She might take a shining to me."

"I doubt it," Davis challenged. "She's a classy woman. She has good taste."

Chapter Eleven

"Hey Caroline," Davis said as he strolled into the familiar café and took his usual seat. Now, however, the view was light years better than usual. Elaine's silky hair was flowing over her shoulders; her piercing blue eyes were glowing brightly. She'd managed to make his sister's old clothes somehow look fashionable again, knotting up the bottom of the flannel shirt and perfectly filling out the cut-off shorts.

"You two are here a little early. You still want the usual?" Caroline asked.

It had become their morning ritual to come to the main strip together, grab a bite to eat at Caroline's, and then both head off to work. Her car hadn't left his driveway since he had it fueled. Being the passenger in his truck, turning that task over to someone else, had been so freeing. She could close her eyes, hang her arm out the window, and trust that he'd keep her safe. Trust that they'd end up right where she wanted to be.

Like they'd been doing it for years, somewhere along the way kissing goodbye had worked itself into the morning ritual. As had holding hands across the table and whispering little jokes that only they knew the punch lines to. It began as teasing the nosy women of the town who loved a juicy piece of gossip.

But now, sitting here across from Elaine, Davis was certain he was falling for her. It was nearly an out of body experience. He could look down on himself and see how absurdly attracted to her he was. How quickly he'd change his plans to make sure they had one more hour together.

"Yes please, Caroline," Elaine answered when Davis, too lost in staring at her, couldn't manage to reply. "Are you all right?"

"Fine," he said, reaching out and covering her tiny hand with his. "I know you're thirty days will be up soon—" She cut him off.

"Let's not think about that right now. I haven't felt this good in a long time. I'm relaxed, I'm happy. I don't want to waste a second wondering what the future holds. I just want to be right here right now with you."

"I can live with that." He smiled. "We don't have to make promises to each other. We don't have to figure it all out. But please, will you consider one thing?"

"I'll try." She shrugged as a waitress filled their coffee mugs and lingered around a long moment, hoping to hear his request. Davis was too patient to fall into that trap. He bit his tongue until she finally moved on.

"When it comes time to decide, when you figure out your next thirty days, try to remember how important it is to feel happy. At some point logic is going to come back into play. You're going to remember you have an apartment in New York and that cutting flowers all day doesn't make much money. Math isn't going to add up, but factor in the way you feel right now."

"I can do that." She beamed, grabbing the warm mug of coffee and lifting it to her lips. She breathed in the smell and closed her eyes. "Caroline's coffee alone could be enough to make me stay. It's the nectar of the gods. I don't know how she does it."

"It's you," Johnny Mildred said as he bumped against their table, nearly knocking their mugs over. "Bill, I told you it was her. Come over here."

Bill Nethers hopped off his chair and approached their table, his beady eyes narrowed as he stared at Elaine. Scrutinizing her in a way that made Davis want to bash him in the head with one of Caroline's fry pans.

"What are you two going on about?" Davis asked, as the heat rose in Elaine's cheeks. She looked mortified and then suddenly afraid. "We're trying to enjoy our morning. Beat it."

"It's the girl from the video; I knew it," Johnny said, slapping Bill's shoulder in victory. "We need to get her picture. Grab my phone off the table."

"No," Elaine pleaded, covering her face with one hand and waving at them to leave with the other. "No, please leave me alone."

"Everyone is looking for you," Bill announced as though Elaine should be as excited as they were. "Just give us a smile. When we post this it'll go viral. We'll all be famous."

"Please leave me alone," she begged again and the desperation in her voice knocked Davis out of his temporary shock and confusion.

"Back off," he barked, shoving his chair backward, sending it to the ground as he stood. "She doesn't want her picture taken. Just go on." He'd known these two guys his whole life. They were hard working fishermen, loud drunks, and always causing someone some annoyance. He'd even scuffled with them a time or two when he was younger, and they'd given him hell when Julie left him for California. Mostly harmless, he figured sticking his chest out and cracking his knuckles would be enough to scare them off. But they were being persistent, and every second that ticked by make Elaine more uncomfortable.

"You've seen the video, haven't you?" Bill asked, still pointing the camera of his phone at Elaine, waiting for a good shot. "It's epic. I laughed for days."

"I won't tell you again," Davis threatened, yanking the phone from Bill's hand and shoving him backward. "You two get out of here. Leave her alone."

"Not a chance," Johnny blustered, backing up a couple steps, but holding his ground once he was out of punching range of Davis. "I'm getting this on video. It'll have a million hits by lunchtime. There's even a hashtag people are using when they think they've spotted you. Who the hell would have thought you'd end up in Indigo Bay? This is incredible."

Caroline slipped between the men and Elaine, her hands propped up on her hips. She'd created a wall of threatening glares and unwavering attitude. "Bill and Johnny, you've got three seconds to get your butts out of my place before I call the sheriff."

"We're not doing anything illegal," Johnny protested, holding his camera phone higher over Caroline's head.

"It's my place, and if I tell you to leave—" Caroline started but Davis was done with this. Whatever was going on, whatever these jerks were talking about, clearly Elaine wanted no part of it. He wasn't going to sit idly by and let them upset her like this.

"Let's go," he said, twisting Johnny's camera-wielding arm behind his back and pulling so tight he cried out in pain.

"You're gonna snap my arm off," he protested as Davis threw him stumbling out the front door. "What's your problem?"

"Are you going out on your own or am I throwing you out too?" Davis asked, closing in on Bill, who looked uneasy about this now that his buddy was not by his side.

"Can I have my phone back?" Bill asked, clearing his throat and putting his hand out expectantly. "It's my property, and you can't keep it. I'll report you for stealing it."

Elaine's eyes were wet with tears as she slouched in the chair, her coffee growing cold, her face falling white as snow suddenly. She looked so small, so weathered by what happened that an anger boiled up in Davis for those who caused this. He threw the phone at Bill, who immediately smiled and took the opportunity to boldly snap a picture of Elaine.

"Give me that," Davis demanded charging at Bill

who dodged him as he clicked away on his phone.

"Too late, it's already been posted," he said smugly. "Everyone will know you're in Indigo Bay now. My social media is going to blow up."

Davis cocked his fist, and pounded Bill in the eye, sending him stumbling backward into the wall. "That was a big mistake," he shouted as he closed in on Bill like a dog charging to a fresh bowl of kibble.

"Davis," Elaine said, her voice shaking, "don't bother. It's too late. He already posted it."

He turned just in time to see her run out of Caroline's and cross the front window. Now he had to choose. Pummel Bill into the bloody unrecognizable heap of garbage he was, or chase after Elaine. "You better hope you don't cross my path again, Bill," Davis said, pointing a threatening finger at him. "You better steer clear of me."

"Go get your girlfriend," Bill shot back as Davis headed toward the door. "If you haven't seen that video, she's got a lot of explaining to do."

Davis was wrong, he could do both. He charged back at Bill and punched him hard in the stomach. When he bent in pain Davis lifted a knee, slamming it into Bill's nose.

"Enough Davis," Caroline demanded. "Go get that girl."

Davis grunted in anger as Bill fell to his knees. Rushing out the front door, he ran in the direction he'd seen Elaine disappear. This road would have taken her back toward his place. To her car. Her getaway car. He knew next to nothing about who Elaine really was. If she drove off today, if she disappeared, there was a chance he'd never see her again.

As much as he didn't want to lose her, he ran back toward his truck, ready to drive every inch of Indigo Bay looking for her, but there was a more pressing question buzzing in his mind.

What the hell was on that video?

Chapter Twelve

Elaine had only felt like this once before. Her chest was as tight as an over-stretched elastic band. Her pulse throbbed so loudly she could hear it in her ears. Maybe it was the running, the way she'd cut toward the ocean and then tumbled down the steep dunes that had her body ready to burst. More likely though it was the fact that everything she'd been hiding from had found her. She had no idea how public her humiliation had become, but in this day in age, she should have known. Nothing received more attention on the internet than someone else's misery.

Originally her plan was to make it back to her car. Davis had filled it with gas, and she could just hit the road and not look back. That's what she'd done when she left New York a couple weeks ago, and it had turned out just fine. There would be another town in another state, and she'd stay there for a while. At least this time she had a little cash in her pocket.

There was only one problem with retrieving her car though. Davis would beat her back there. He'd be standing there, arms folded across his chest, looking for answers she didn't want to give. It was hard enough to believe strangers had seen what had happened. Once Davis knew, he'd never look at her the same way. Those slow mornings at the café would be over. The late nights talking under the stars would vanish. She certainly hadn't been able to look at herself the same since it had happened, so Davis couldn't be blamed for that.

Instead of taking a chance on bumping into Davis, she'd walk the shoreline south. Once she was out of Indigo Bay, she'd hitchhike. When she got where she was going she would have someone send her purse and credit cards. It was crazy what she'd been doing here. Living without touching her savings just because she didn't want anyone to know where she was. They'd know now. That picture of her at Caroline's, tears in her eyes and shame on her face, was going to be plastered all over the internet soon. This thing she was doing in Indigo Bay, this pretend life, was silly. She would close out the lease on her apartment, hire a company to move everything out, and she'd have her doorman ship her purse and all its contents to her new location. The savings she stashed away would be more than enough to sustain her. She could still live this life far from New York, but she'd need to get her affairs in order. Davis had made it too easy for her to live in limbo. To pretend. She could still pull this off, she'd just have to do it without the one thing that seemed to make it all worthwhile. Davis.

As she lifted her hand to her hair, which was being blown in all directions by the ocean air, she caught a waft of his scent on her fingers. Just a little while ago their hands had been laced together. Just a little while ago, he was looking at her in a way no one else ever had. There was an honesty in Davis, a genuine and impressive amount of character she'd never come across before. Her first night in Indigo Bay, Caroline had said he was one of the best men she'd known, and she trusted him wholeheartedly. Elaine had come to see how easy it was to believe.

She was falling for Davis. His strong shoulders, his easy gentle voice, and his unique ability to make her think deeper than she wanted to. He was a man who, under different circumstances, she could have seen herself falling in love with. The problem was she knew his past. He'd shared it with her, and here she was making him repeat it. Elaine would be just another woman to sweep Davis up in her wake and then coldly leave him behind. It was better she was going now. She'd tamp down all her own desire and the comfort she found while with him and give him the gift he deserved, her absence.

After about an hour she'd come to the edge of Indigo Bay. Her shoes were full of sand. Her hair was tangled and loaded with knots from the wind. All the cottages and tiny oceanfront restaurants were behind her, and a long stretch of shore with nothing on it lay before her. Stopping abruptly, she turned around and took in the scene she'd just walked through. As the waves lapped gently on the shore and the gulls dove headlong toward their dinner, she drew in a deep breath. Her stomach rumbled with hunger as the sun grew higher in the sky. All she wanted right now was some of Caroline's cobbler, two spoons, and the best man she ever knew to share it with.

Chapter Thirteen

"You can't file a missing persons case on her and you know it," Paul said as he leaned back in his chair and threw his legs up on the desk. "A girl can leave town whenever she wants. I know you two were getting hot and heavy, but I can't chase down every chick who leaves you. I'd have to get some serious overtime on that one."

Davis ground his teeth together. Paul was the one guy on the force he couldn't stand and always seemed to be throwing digs his way. "She left without her car. She's walking somewhere on her own. She's upset. I'm worried about her."

"Makes sense since the last girl you chased out of here didn't wind up doing too well in the grand scheme of things. Your worry is likely justified."

Bringing up Julie's accident was over the line. "If you think that badge is going to keep me from pounding your head in then you have gravely misjudged me," Davis boomed, slamming a hand down on the desk and shoving Paul's feet to the ground.

"Easy fellas," Dallas said coolly, his hands tucked casually into his pockets. "My buddy Davis and I were just leaving. No need to grab those handcuffs, Paul."

Dallas gestured with his head for Davis to follow

him outside, and it took all his willpower to do so without taking a quick shot at Paul on the way by.

"That's assaulting an officer you know," Dallas said, holding the door open to make sure Davis was actually going to leave. When they hit the street Davis felt the urge to run.

"I've got to go man. I've got to look for her." Davis felt his friend's hand clamp down on his shoulder before he could hurry away.

"We've known each other a long time," Dallas began, and Davis nearly interrupted, not wanting the lecture. But Dallas didn't look like he'd take no for an answer. "I was with you when you fell in love with Julie. I was here every single time that girl stomped on your heart."

"This is different," Davis insisted.

"I know it is," Dallas nodded. "Because you're different. And from what I've seen of Elaine, she's a nice girl. My mom really took a shine to her, you two eating breakfast there together every morning. Having us up to your house for dinner. It's been something, and I can tell how happy you are. She does a nice job for Mrs. Donavan at the florist shop, too."

"I need to go find her," Davis demanded, shaking free of his grip. "We're wasting time. She's upset, and she's off walking to who knows where right now."

"You think it's normal that a girl shows up here the way she does and then takes off the way she just did today? She left her car sitting in your driveway just so she wouldn't have to face you. What does that tell you?"

"It tells me she's upset about something. I can help."

Dallas shook his head in disagreement. "It tells you she's hurting, and she's not wanting you to see her right now. Maybe give her a little space."

"Bill and Johnny," Davis said, spinning on Dallas quickly so they were staring each other in the eye, "said there was some kind of video. I don't want to know about it. I don't want to see it."

"Fair enough," Dallas assured him. "I've heard the whispers about it after this morning, but you know I'm the last person around here to be checking my social media every minute. I think that's why she stayed here as long as she did, Indigo Bay is isolated. It was easy for her to go unnoticed here for a while."

"She should have told me what was going on," Davis grunted as they started walking again. "I'd have understood. There's nothing she could have done that would change my opinion of her."

"Well," Dallas said, clearing his throat, "I wouldn't go committing to that. Give it some time. I saw how she was looking at you. I saw how she smiled every time you came in a room. I don't think she'll be able to just run off, and that's the end of it. But chasing her might make things worse."

"I just want to know she's fine," Davis groaned, running his hands through his hair in frustration. "We didn't make any promises to each other. It's not like there were future plans. But I want to know she is somewhere safe. When I found her that night, she was a mess."

"And she was damn lucky it was here, and it was

you. Who knows where she could have ended up if not. I hear what you're saying. I'd be worried too." Dallas fished his keys out of his pocket and looked thoughtfully down the road. "You said you drove this road all the way south for ten miles? No sign of her?"

"No, and I drove north the same distance. If she were on the road, I'd have seen her. She couldn't have gotten farther than that on foot in this amount of time.

"So maybe someone else picked her up?" Dallas said, wringing his hands as he gave it some serious thought. "I don't like the idea of her hopping in the car with just anyone."

"I hope not," Davis said, shaking his head. "Lots of people pass through here. Truckers, transient people of all kinds. I'd hate to think she was so desperate to get away from me that she hopped in the car with someone who had less than admirable intentions for her."

"I'm sure she'd be on her guard," Dallas offered, but it sounded hollow. "She might be upset, but I think she's a sharp girl. She wouldn't get in just any car."

"If something happens to her because she couldn't face me," Davis edged out. "If she felt like she needed to run from here just because of what I would think, I can't live with that. I can't live with another woman—"

"Don't make me knock your lights out right now," Dallas said, cocking his fist back. "You don't get to put all of this on you. I've spent too many years watching you do that. This is different. Elaine and

Julie are nothing alike. She's going to be fine. I have an idea."

Dallas hopped in his truck and rolled down the window. "If she wasn't on the road and didn't hop a ride with someone, maybe she walked down the shoreline. I'll go to the cabins and get the four-wheeler. I'll drive it south, down the shoreline and see if I can spot her."

"I'll come too," Davis said, relieved to at least have a plan.

"No," Dallas said, quickly pushing the lock button before Davis could reach for the handle to let himself in. "Go back to your place in case she comes back. Keep yourself busy. I'll call you if I see her. I don't intend to bother her; I'm not going to plead your case to her. I'll let you know if she's doing fine or not."

"You're a good friend, Dallas," Davis said, patting the hood of the car as he backed out. It killed him to be left behind, but if Elaine showed up at the cabin he wanted to be there.

"I raised a pretty good boy," Caroline said, rounding the corner and tucking her hands into the pockets of her overalls. There was an easiness about her that Davis always craved in moments like this. She could give advice or sit quietly in support. But what made her special was knowing exactly when to do which. "My boys have good friends too. We certainly lucked out with you staying here in Indigo Bay all this time. I know how many times you've helped Dallas. I know how often he relies on you. I'm glad he can be around to pay back the favor. Though I don't really appreciate when you have fistfights in my café."

"I'm sorry about that," Davis apologized, running his hand over his brow and kicking a stone by his foot. Caroline could make him feel twelve years old again. She might as well have been scolding him for taking a cookie from the jar. "I shouldn't have hit him. I know violence is not the answer."

"I didn't say that," Caroline corrected, wearing a wry smile. "Those guys were asking for it. But I wouldn't have minded if you'd dragged him outside first. There's always next time."

"Right," Davis grinned, grateful for her forgiveness and the levity in a moment where everything around him felt as though it were crumbling.

"Do you know what that was all about this morning?" Caroline asked as they began to walk down toward the water. "I know you two were getting close, but you looked blindsided.

"I was," he groaned, embarrassed to have to admit the woman he was falling in love with also happened to be a stranger to him. "Apparently she's famous, or infamous I should say. The guys this morning, they saw her on some kind of video. I don't know what's on it; I just know Bill and Johnny felt compelled to post about it. Some kind of big deal, I guess. She clearly didn't want anyone to know. She was spooked. I reacted to what I thought she wanted."

"I never liked social media. Mostly because it doesn't seem to be either of those words. They should call it mobile distraction that's essentially negative."

“Doesn’t exactly roll off the tongue.” Davis chuckled, filling his lungs with the sea air and wishing he’d asked Elaine more questions along the way. If he’d have pressed for the truth earlier, he could have protected her from this. Or he could have protected himself from losing her.

“You control everything,” Caroline explained, patting his back maternally, “or at least you try. I know you have been keeping yourself shut off from the world, and you finally let someone in. Don’t let this derail you. I liked seeing how happy you were with her. Elaine is a lovely girl. If she ends up being the woman you sit across from and smile that big smile, wonderful. If she doesn’t, don’t tuck that happiness away for quite so long this next time.”

“I’m only sorry she didn’t feel like she could tell me what was going on. Didn’t she trust me to help her?” Davis felt his muscles tense as he remembered Elaine darting out of the café like a spooked rabbit whose twitching ears had picked up the rumbles of impending danger.

“It’s not a lack of trust in you that kept her quiet,” Caroline corrected. “It’s the scary idea that something might change when you see that part of her. At the beginning, when you’re just starting out with someone, you know how it is. It’s all the shiny parts. Having something out of your control force you away from the joyful beginning part of a relationship is downright unfair. I’m sure she believes something she’s done might be the reason she loses you.”

“I don’t cut and run,” Davis said, knowing he was defending himself to the wrong person. Caroline had seen him grow up, and in turn, she'd been witness to every piece of him being slid into place. During every phase he awkwardly passed through, she was there on the sideline, cheering. Watching. Even sometimes wincing. "I can deal with the tough stuff; she just has to give me a chance."

"You don't cut and run," Caroline smiled, her face oozing with the obvious irony. "But she does. You've got to make peace with that and figure out what that means for you. It's who she is right now. A runner. So now what?"

"I have no idea." Davis sighed as they stepped down the long path onto the sand. "For the first time in a long time I have no idea what tomorrow is going to bring. That's frustrating."

"No son, that's exciting."

Chapter Fourteen

Dallas's car pulled up outside, and his headlights hit the bright purple cabin. Davis had planted himself on the porch swing with no intention of going to bed that night. The arrival of his friend, and whatever pestering came along with it, wouldn't change that. Sleep was for the peaceful. The happy. Sleep was not for tormented men who'd let the best woman they'd ever known slip away.

"Did you find her?" he asked, popping to his feet and flying down the steps of the porch. "Any sign of her?"

"Yep," Dallas said, pulling off his baseball hat and fidgeting with the brim. "She's all right. She made it about seven miles down the beach, and I saw her going in the front door of a bed and breakfast. Looks like she's staying there tonight. I asked about her in the little seafood shack, and a waitress said she was on the phone with someone, asking them to ship her purse and a few of her belongings."

"Ship them to the bed and breakfast?" Davis asked, his voice loaded with excitement. "That's good then. She'll be there at least a few days. Which place is it?"

"Doesn't matter," Dallas said firmly. "Let her be for a while. It's not like she's really going to just leave her perfectly good car right here. Let her get her stuff and give her some time to cool off."

"She could come for her car while I'm at work. Then who knows where she would end up? I'd really lose her then."

"Don't you think maybe that's a sign?" Dallas offered. "If she's ready to leave you in her dust, maybe you should let her."

"If she doesn't care about me, I'm fine with that," he lied. "But what I won't do is let her run away because she's worried about what I think. If the only reason she's not here is because she can't face me, I want to deal with that head on. I'll look her in the eye, and if she doesn't feel the way I do, I'll let her walk away."

"Fine," Dallas said, tossing his hands up in defeat and looking unconvinced. "But not tonight. Not tomorrow either. Give her at least that. I think it'll be better that way."

"And I'm supposed to just sit here?" Davis asked, gesturing over to the porch swing. "I'm off work the next two days, so what am I supposed to do?"

"For heaven's sake, man," Dallas scolded. "Do something for you. Do something that isn't work, or sleep, or exercising. Try to remember back when life was easy, and you weren't trying to fill up every second just so you don't have to feel anything. Do that for a couple days and maybe you'll both be in better shape when you talk."

"When did you get so deep and insightful?" Davis asked, climbing back up the steps and sinking into the cushions of the porch swing. He couldn't help but cast a sarcastic look at Dallas, whose face was red with frustration. "I feel like you actually have your act together now."

"Oh yeah." He laughed and rolled his eyes. "I'm thinking of launching my own talk show any day now. Just tell me you have beer in the fridge and that my mom sent you home with some cookies or something."

"Yep, help yourself," Davis said, gesturing into the cabin. "No one knows how to heal a broken heart like your mom and her baked goods. It's the least I can do for all the sage wisdom you're offering me."

"That's true," Dallas called from the kitchen. "As a matter of fact I'm taking some of these leftovers, too. I'm on point with this advice, and it makes me hungry. Being brilliant burns calories."

Davis closed his eyes and listened intently to the crashing waves at the foot of the dunes. He had bought this place from Dallas as a gift for Julie. He'd painted it purple to win her over, to convince her to stay. The guy who had done all that, who had become nearly unrecognizable to himself just to persuade a woman he loved to stay, was gone. Davis wasn't that kid anymore. He knew love was not a trap you set in hopes of snaring an unsuspecting heart.

He was different. Elaine was not Julie. And this was not a high school love he'd hung on to like favorite shirt long since outgrown. There was a spark between him and Elaine. An abstract connection that couldn't be summed up easily, which was a scary prospect. But it also couldn't be quickly swept aside and forgotten. His only hope was that she felt the same way about what they'd shared. If not, he'd let her go.

Chapter Fifteen

The bed was rock hard. The pipes rattled in the walls. It was too hot, but with the window open, too cold. Elaine could think up a thousand excuses for why she couldn't sleep, but they were just that. Excuses. The real reason her eyes wouldn't stay shut was because etched on the back of her lids was the contents of a video she couldn't outrun. Even in sleepy Indigo Bay. Davis had seemed to be so shocked by how cruel the world outside his little town could be. Elaine, on the other hand, knew what a cut throat world it was out there. Especially in her career field. All it took was someone wanting what you had and it could be snatched away in the blink of an eye.

She'd fallen prey to that. Letting her own guard down, she was swept up in the lies she normally would have been able to see right through. She'd forgotten the best advice she'd been given: being kind doesn't guarantee you kindness in return. It only increases your odds of being betrayed.

The pipes rattled again, and Elaine wished she were back at Davis's perfectly quiet purple cabin. Being with him was more than just an escape from the things that had hurt her. It was the first time in her life she'd felt completely relaxed. Calm. At peace. Every moment together they were the only thing that mattered. Somewhere along the way she realized the stress she'd packed onto her life wasn't the result of growing up. It wasn't a natural consequence she had to deal with. She'd burdened herself with goals for a life she'd imagined, stacking more and more weight on her already sinking body. And out of nowhere, Davis had cracked his knuckles, bent his knees, and lifted it all off her body. A wonderful gift, but temporary. Now she was faced with saddling herself once more with the reality of what she'd done.

Pulling the itchy blanket over her face, she let the tears drip down her chin. How could running away be so easy and so terribly difficult all at once?

Chapter Sixteen

Elaine knew Davis would be home. It wouldn't have been hard to wait one more day for him to go to work and try to avoid him. But that wasn't what she wanted. He deserved better than that. She expected to find him tinkering on a boat engine, or watching a game on television, but what she found was far more surprising.

"You're painting?" she asked, folding her arms nervously across her body as if the solo hug might keep her from imploding. Davis was on a ladder with a brush in his hand and a bucket of white paint balanced at the top. The purple on the front of the cabin was nearly gone, eaten up by stark white with every stroke from his brush.

"The purple wasn't really me," Davis said, not turning around to see her. "I thought it was time to make this place my own again."

"It looks good," she said, feeling utterly exposed and self-conscious. "I'm sorry I ran off. You deserve better than that. You deserve the truth."

"You don't owe me a thing, Elaine," Davis said, still focused solely on the job at hand. "If you don't feel for me what I do for you, I'm not going to chase you."

"You might not feel anything for me once you know more about me," she croaked out, wondering if she should just hop in her car and drive away. Running. Instant gratification, poor long-term strategy, she reminded herself.

Davis's hand froze, the brush mid-stroke as he shook his head. "Give me a little more credit than that. I'm not those guys in Sweet Caroline's the other morning. I'm not someone from New York you used to know. At least give me a chance before you decide how I'll feel about something."

"You're right," she stuttered apologetically. "I'm embarrassed. I'm scared. I don't want to lose you." As though she'd been standing in front of a locked door, uttering every magic phrase she could think of, she finally hit the right one. Davis dropped the brush into the bucket of paint and made his way hastily down the ladder. When he reached the bottom, he stared at her as though he needed to hear it again, so she obliged. "I just don't want to lose you." Like an antsy horse let out of the gate, he ran to her.

His lips crushed hers as he lifted her off her feet. She might have winced under his tight grip had she not been clinging equally as hard to him.

"You won't lose me," he breathed, breaking the kiss but keeping their lips just centimeters apart. "Come inside."

His hand was in hers, leading her toward the door when she tugged back a bit. "Davis," she started then stopped abruptly, looking over her shoulder nervously. Her car was there. Escape was within reach. But it wasn't what she wanted anymore.

Davis shook his head and continued to lead her into the house. "Elaine, this cabin is my sanctuary.

I've hidden here on my darkest days. I hardly let anyone in. These walls have saved me." They sank into the plush cushions of the couch, and he held her hands reassuringly. "When you're in here, no matter what you're worried about, it can't get you. Nothing and no one comes through that door unless I let them. I don't think anyone should spend their life hiding out, but I think everyone deserves a place they can hide once in a while. Let this be your place. I'll be the gatekeeper. I'll be the one who keeps everything you're worried about at bay. Just let me do that for you. This house is the safest place you could be."

She lost her breath as the emotion welled inside her. Suddenly the half purple cabin felt like a fortress. Visions of a crocodile-filled moat, a big steel gate, and high stone walls crept into her mind. In here there was no New York. There were no mistakes. Only Davis's large warm arms promising her protection. "Davis, how can you so blindly believe in me?"

"I have no idea who you were before this. Maybe I wouldn't have liked that woman very much. Who knows? But I know who you are now. I saw you sitting on the curb that night, a broken spirit, and I watched you put yourself back together. You might think I did everything to help you, but you are the one who put one foot in front of the other every day. You were ready to give up, and you didn't. That's someone I can believe in."

"I'm a coward." She sighed, her head falling into her hands. "I literally ran away from my life."

"Tell me why," he said, his voice gentle and as welcoming as an overfilled pillow and warm sheets at the end of a long day. "You can tell me."

"I was fired," she replied, knowing that was a very small tip of an enormous iceberg she was about to expose. "I broke ethics rules at work, and I was very publicly fired."

"Oh," Davis said, his face reading unimpressed, almost let down by the revelation. "Are you in legal trouble because of it?"

"No," she shot back quickly. "I didn't break any laws. I would never do that. I handle client's entire futures. I wouldn't be able to live with myself if I broke the law."

"Then what?" Davis asked, lifting her chin upward and out of her hands so he could see her better. "It doesn't sound that bad. Losing your job must have been a real blow, but you could get another job, right? I don't mean to dismiss how you're feeling. It must have been hard."

"I was very successful," she started, the pang of regret raging in her stomach like a bottle of soda that had been shaken for days. "I dedicated every minute of my life to advancing through the ranks, even though the odds weren't in my favor. Most people in my position had a pedigree, a family who gave them opportunities. My father was a disgraced businessman. I had to fight against his reputation instead of benefit from it. But clients liked me. They trusted me, and I was making them a fortune. I was making my firm a fortune. I couldn't believe how close I was to reaching my dreams. But I screwed up. I fell for a guy."

"And he broke your heart?" Davis asked, pursing

his lips as though the idea of another man, especially one that hurt her, didn't drive him crazy.

"It's more complicated than that. I'd like to believe I could deal with a simple broken heart. I made the mistake of letting my guard down. I was mentoring a woman who'd just graduated from college. She got wind of my success, and her dad was a powerful guy. He set it up for me to coach her. When you spend that much time together you become friends. We had a lot in common, and she was really nice to me. I liked her. Elizabeth was what I thought I'd been missing for years. A good, reliable friend. One day I risked sharing a secret with her. I told her I was dating Mick Lawrence."

"Your boss?" Davis asked, jumping to a pretty reasonable but misguided conclusion.

"No," she said, shaking her head. "Have you ever heard the term Chinese Wall?"

"No," Davis said, furrowing his brow to try to dissect the term.

"I hate the term and don't use it myself. It's one of those lingering terms people still throw around, but I think it's offensive. There's a lot of that antiquated garbage in this industry. Once I explain it, you'll see what I mean."

"I'll try to keep up," Davis assured her.

"Mick was technically my peer, though he'd been in the business longer. At a firm like ours they call the rule that should block insider or privileged information a Chinese Wall. It's essentially an information barrier. I worked on one side and Mick on the other. I held the information about what deals were coming down the line that could be very lucrative. I dealt with equity research, investor relations with potential clients and running models to determine how a stock or company might perform. Does that make sense?"

"Uh," Davis said, his brow still furrowed, "for the purposes of this conversation I think I'm following you. It's like a referee in a basketball game doesn't get to bet on the outcome. You don't get to make the calls and benefit from it. There's no way to be impartial that way."

"Right. That's a good way to think about it. I'm frequently in a position to advise a company outside of my firm about merging or taking over another company. That would dramatically influence future stock prices and disseminating that information to someone like Mick would not be legal. It's an unfair advantage because the facts are not yet known to the public. Being in a relationship with someone on the other side of that wall isn't illegal, but it's ethically wrong."

"You can't help who you fall for I guess," Davis said, muddling through the part of the conversation that implied she was once in love with Mick enough to jeopardize her career.

"I thought it was getting pretty serious between us, and I wasn't sure what to do. Our firm has a non-negotiable no-fraternizing clause we all sign when we get hired. We hold a lot of power in our hands every day and interpersonal relationships can cloud judgment. It can muddy water even if we all act in a technically legal way. But Mick assured me the first few times we went out that people didn't take that clause seriously. He named a bunch of people who'd been in relationships in the office and never had any trouble. I guess you believe what you want when you're starting a relationship. Sure, he told me we had to keep it a secret, but that was only until we knew where it was heading. If we became serious we'd go to our boss and work out some solution. I told Elizabeth I thought it was time we do that. Mick had told me he loved me earlier that week. I assumed our boss would have to work with human resources and then likely restructure our department so Mick and I didn't have any conflicts of interest. He told me it had been done before for others."

"Would you have to step back from your job?" Davis asked, and whether he meant it or not she felt the heat of judgment rolling up her neck.

"A little bit, probably. Mick had been there longer. He was very successful for the firm, in a different capacity than I was. But I thought we had a real future, so I was willing to do it if that was what it took. We never had the chance to talk to our boss though. What I didn't know when I was confiding in Elizabeth was that she and Mick were dating too. I don't think she knew about us before I told her. I certainly didn't know about them. From that moment on, she started working on taking me down."

"Taking you down? How exactly does someone do that? And why? It's not like you were the one stealing this jerk from her. He was who needed to be taken down." She could feel Davis tense up, holding his breath for long moments as if to keep from saying too much.

"Maybe," Elaine agreed. "But I was, by far, the easier target. So she made a video. Acting like she was utterly fascinated with my blossoming relationship, she asked me a ton of questions, and I answered them, sounding like a lovesick puppy, explaining exactly where we were when he said he loved me. I told her everything, the way you'd tell a best friend at a sleepover. Mostly because I'd been so isolated and so focused on work that I'd missed what it meant to connect with someone. I was easy to fool because I was out of practice."

"Did she play the video for your boss?" Davis asked, looking angry on her behalf.

"That would have been far kinder than what she actually did. If I could have signed up for a private viewing of my humiliation, I would have. Apparently she minored in video production. She turned my relationship with Mick into a short movie where I was the idiot who had no clue he was also dating Elizabeth. But more than that, he was using me. The way Mick became successful over the years was exactly what he was doing with me. He convinced women they had to keep their relationship a secret. He acted like a mentor, but he was soliciting client information and angles from me. I was giving away minor information without knowing how he could spin it and use it to his advantage. Elizabeth recorded him at lunch with two of my biggest clients, who were on the verge of taking their company public. There was only a small circle of people who would have known about their plans. I never technically told him what was happening, but he pieced together pretty innocuous conversations of ours and figured out the important stuff. You could do that when you spent so much time together, when the other person had their guard down. No laws were broken. Elizabeth strung all that together so perfectly it was like a cinematic masterpiece. She could have won an award for it."

"Why would anyone spend that much energy trying to hurt someone else?" Davis asked, his teeth grinding together in rage.

"Every Friday morning the firm has a meeting," Elaine continued, knowing the worst part of the story wasn't over. "The entire office stands on the floor of the assembly room, and we put our numbers up for the week. It's competitive and it's motivational. Elizabeth switched out the numbers for her movie. She played it for all fifty-two of my coworkers, my boss, and the president of the company, who happened to be in that day. It was four minutes and twenty-seven seconds long but every single second of it felt like a stab wound. I couldn't breathe. Every person in the room stared at me. Mick started out angry, demanding someone take it down, then after seeing how it painted him, he and a few of his buddies began laughing. That was my breaking point."

"I'd like to get my hands on that guy," Davis said, his hands balled into fists. "Who would let you just stand there and be destroyed like that?"

"The president of the company looked over the crowd and asked who was in the video. I was too shocked to raise my hand, but luckily my long-time coworkers had no problem pointing me out. In a booming voice he called me a disgrace to the company, a woman with no moral standings, and an employee with no credibility. He made an example of me, berating me a few more minutes and then telling me to get out."

"What?" Davis asked, shooting to his feet. "That is insane. You are the victim here."

"I broke the rules. I should never have discussed private client information with Mick, no matter how small it was. I should have never been involved with him on a personal level. I knew those things, and I did them anyway."

"Because you trusted him." Davis was pacing now, his legs fueled by indignation. "You could have a lawsuit on your hands. I mean this guy, Mick . . . he must not have been laughing when he was fired."

"He wasn't fired," Elaine breathed out, with a humorless laugh. "His uncle is the CFO of another prominent company my firm frequently works with. Before I made it out the door, someone came and told me he would get a slap on the wrist, but he wouldn't be fired. He was too valuable. Which in turn made me completely valueless, apparently."

"That's not true," Davis replied quickly. "This entire situation is screwed up. There has to be something you can do. Fight it."

"I probably could," Elaine agreed, raising her brows high and considering it. "But for what? Those people are connected to other firms. I'd never get another job in New York even if I cleared all this up.

And I don't want one anyway. I don't want to go back to that lifestyle. It was crippling. I didn't realize it until I was out of it. Until I was sitting on your porch listening to the far away thunder, watching fireflies whizz by. I didn't know how fast I was going, how close I was to crashing until I got to Indigo Bay and slowed down."

"So the video was leaked onto the internet," Davis said, connecting all the remaining dots. "That's how those boneheads in Sweet Caroline's knew about you?"

"Worse," she said, dropping her head, not wanting to look at him. "It was re-edited to include my dismissal. Being yelled at. Mick laughing. And me running out of the building like an idiot. That's the version that's on the internet. I was trying not to face it, but I finally had my doorman ship my things here. When I turned my phone back on today I saw the video had over a million hits. Reading some of the comments, I can tell you, no one is rooting for me."

"Every word I said when you first came in here stands true. Nothing out there matters. I can keep it all as far away as you want me to. You're safe here. I know the truth, and I know you didn't deserve any of that."

"Those guys at the cafe posted a picture of me and said where I was. There are all kinds of hashtags and stuff. My phone came in the package from the doorman and I have 100 voice mails from internet sites and bloggers who want to talk to me. If I stay in Indigo Bay, they'll turn this place into a circus. I don't want to do that to you."

"The only thing you can do to me that I won't be able to handle is leave me. If you really want to be with me, if you want to make a life here, then we face this together."

Davis reached for his ringing cell phone and saw it was Dallas. He'd missed two calls from him already and figured he better check in. "Hey what's up?" he asked, popping it to speaker phone. "I'm in the middle of something right now if it can wait."

"It can't," Dallas cut in. "You need to go get Elaine from the bed and breakfast. The town is swarming with people looking for her, and I'm afraid someone is going to tip them off to where she is. You don't want this group spooking her."

"She's here with me." Davis smiled, looking bashful for having known where she was the past couple of days. "I don't care how many people try to get to her. They don't stand a chance." He disconnected the call and closed in on Elaine, who was shaking with emotion.

"You knew where I was these last couple of days?" she asked, as his arms wrapped around her. She pressed her ear to his chest and listened to his steady heartbeat.

"I wanted to give you some space," he admitted. "It was killing me, not going down there and begging you to tell me what you were going through. But I had faith you'd show up here."

"What if I ran? What if I snuck over, got my car, and you never saw me again?" Elaine asked, swallowing back the lump in her throat.

"Then I'd know you weren't right for me," he

admitted somberly. "The one lesson in my life I'll never be forced to learn again, is how easy it is to confuse the chase with real emotions. When someone leaves, everything feels more intense. The rejection creates this hole in you. The real crime is you start to believe that hole they left is shaped like them, that they are the only one who can fill it completely. That's the lie we tell ourselves. The one who left, them coming back, is the only way to get better. There's a million ways to get better."

"But I came back," she said, squeezing him tightly.

"And somehow, I knew you would."

Chapter Seventeen

Davis put another log on the fire and stoked it until embers flew toward the night sky. “Dallas called and said most folks have moved on. Your story will be old news in no time. Someone else will do something slightly more interesting, and they’ll be chasing that story. Then you can get on with your life. I’m sure you’ll have stuff to sort out.”

“I have to go back and close up my apartment, but other than that I’m free and clear. I have my credit cards now and access to all my savings. I can do anything I need to do.” She pulled the blanket tighter over her shoulders as the wind picked up.

“Should we go back inside?” Davis asked. “Is it getting too cold for you?”

“I’m fine,” she assured him, patting the sand next to her so he would sit. “You can keep me warm.”

“A job I’d sign up for every day.” He sat, wrapped his arm around her, and kissed the crown of her head. “Are you sure you’re not going to miss any of it? Indigo Bay is about as different from your old life as it gets. Don’t you think you should give it all more thought? You went through a lot, and maybe you’re just having a gut reaction to the stress. I don’t want to be too influential if you have regrets.”

“You’ll just have to make sure I never regret it,” she said, laying her head on his shoulder. “Sounds like a lot of work but I bet you're up to the challenge."

"I'm being serious, Elaine," Davis replied, the thought that had been snaking through his mind all afternoon finally slithering out. "Obviously, I've already told you how I feel about you. But more important than anything is that you find exactly what you need to be happy. Feeling trapped in Indigo Bay isn't any better than feeling stressed in New York. I want you to be sure about your choices. We can figure everything else out afterward."

"A long distance relationship between Indigo Bay and Alaska maybe?" she teased, her pearl white teeth lighting her face. "I like it here, Davis. I like the people. I can be happy here."

"You won't miss anything about New York?" he pressed, and he could feel her body growing rigid. It was either a sign he was pushing the topic too far or he was right.

"That's not really fair. Of course I'll miss things there. I lived there my whole life. Anyone moving away would feel that way. But that doesn't mean I'm not capable of making a sound choice for what I do next. I'm not closing my eyes and diving in. I've given it a lot of thought. I guess I have to take responsibility that you might doubt me. The way I arrived doesn't give me much credibility. You'll just have to trust that I'm thinking clearly now."

"I do," he said, rubbing a hand up and down her back gently. "I'm sorry. I do trust that. I'm just a bit jumpy when it comes to girls I love and the big cities that lure them away."

"The girls you love?" she asked, pulling away and glaring nervously at him. "You can't be saying that you—"

He cut her off. "Easy bolt, don't go making a break for it. I wasn't trying to spook you. You don't have to say it back. I was just letting you know. When I feel like this for someone, and there is another world they can easily run off to, it's a challenge for me. I'm asking you to give me a little grace."

"Davis?" A voice from atop the dunes was shouting frantically. "Davis, are you down there? Is Elaine with you?"

"Caroline?" Davis asked, jumping to his feet and pulling Elaine up. "What's the matter?"

"It's Dallas, he's been detained by the police. He told me to come here and warn you and Elaine." Caroline's voice was a jumble of high and even higher octaves as she waved for them to hurry.

Davis was charging up the dunes, practically dragging Elaine behind him. He knew both Dallas and Caroline well enough to know this urgency shouldn't be ignored. "Warn us about what?"

"It's Elaine's ex, Mick, he's here. He was banging on every door in town looking for her. When he got to some of the cabins, Dallas didn't want him on his property and told him to move on. But he was insisting. He kept banging on every door, and Dallas called the sheriff."

"Then how did he get detained?" Davis asked, fumbling for his car keys. "Shouldn't Mick be locked up right now for disturbing the peace?"

"They took too long to get there. That's what

happens in a town with only a couple of deputies on duty. There were some media guys still hanging around, and they were trying to get them to move along. They were busy. Dallas took matters into his own hands."

"Did he hit the guy?" Davis asked, doing a terrible job of hiding his excitement.

"Worse," Caroline groaned. "He rammed his truck into the guy's sports car. He says it was an accident. This Mick guy says it was intentional. I think they'll sort it out just fine, but Dallas wanted me to tell you guys to go to the cabin in the woods he was originally going to set Elaine up in. The roof's been repaired, and you can stay there until this guy moves on."

"I'm not worried about him at all," Davis said, puffing up his chest. He was itching for a fight. "If he's got a problem I'm happy to solve it for him and send him on his way."

"I don't think Dallas was worried about you handling yourself," Caroline corrected. "I think he was far more concerned with you becoming his cell mate. You don't need any trouble. Just steer clear."

"Does that sound like me?" Davis asked, reaching for the door handle of his truck. "It's like you don't know me at all."

"I do know you," Caroline said, planting a hand on the hood of the truck. "Which is why I'm going to make you run me over before I let you go down there."

"Davis," Elaine interrupted, catching her breath. "I want to go down and talk to Mick alone. I don't want you getting involved."

"I'm already involved. He messed with you, and that makes it my problem too. Now Dallas could be caught up in this. I'm going to go straighten it out right now."

"When I first got here," she reminded him, a challenging brow raised, "you told me I didn't need a knight to come fight my battles. I needed a sword. I was rattled. I was hurt, but I'm seeing clearly now. I need to do this on my own. If you swoop in and try to save me, it'll only get worse. A couple of guys fighting over a woman who isn't even torn between them. Mick means nothing to me. Let me go tell him that."

"The guy sounds unstable. He's walking around town, banging on doors looking for you." Davis wasn't sure how much he believed his own warning. He pictured Mick as a beady eyed rat-faced kind of guy with slim shoulders and slicked back hair. Probably on the short side too. The guy probably never dressed in anything more casual than a suit and flashed wads of money the way Davis carried his old worn thin leather wallet with a couple twenties in it for emergencies. Unstable or not, he believed Elaine could handle herself. Hearing about her job, her fight to gain her spot in the world, surely she could kick one slimeball to the curb on her own. So why was he still insisting? Realizing, his cheeks grew hot. It was the worry that she might not dismiss him at all.

"Dallas smashed his truck into his car, and we're worried Mick is the unstable one? We're giving out a lot of passes tonight." Elaine tried to soften her words with a touch to his arm and a tiny smile. Although they both knew there was no humor in this situation.

"You want to talk to him alone, fine. I won't say a word, but I'm still going with you. I won't interfere unless he pulls something stupid." Davis was a good guy but even he was hoping Mick tried something stupid. All he could picture was the vision of Mick snickering in the corner while Elaine's world fell in around her.

"I think he might have been drunk," Caroline warned, looking reluctant to fuel the fire. "He was definitely agitated, and that was before Dallas wrecked his car."

"He's harmless," Elaine sighed, tipping her head to the side and giving Davis a knowing look. "You have to trust me."

"Caroline," Davis said, hopping in the driver's seat, "I'm going to stay out of the way, you've got my word. Now don't make me run you over."

"Boy"—she laughed waggling her finger at him—"you know I'm tougher than nails. I'd turn this truck over with my bare hands. Then I'd tie you to that porch swing."

Elaine laughed as she slid into the passenger seat of his truck.

"I wouldn't laugh," Davis corrected. "I've seen her do some wild things."

"And I'm not above punishing you if you break your word," she said as she stepped back and let him pass.

"Thanks for coming up here," Davis said warmly as Caroline circled around to his window and touched his shoulder.

"You handle your business now, girl," she said, pointing at Elaine, "and make sure this guy doesn't wind up in a bunk bed with my son in a holding cell."

"Yes ma'am," Elaine promised as they pulled away.

"He does one thing," Davis ground out, his grip on the steering wheel growing tighter by the second. "Why would he chase you down here if he was just using you? It doesn't make sense. How can someone be so complicit in you getting hurt, so dead set on taking advantage of you, and in the next breath be looking all over the place for you? Is there something you aren't telling me?"

"In a little while it won't matter. He'll be gone. You and I will be back at your house. I can start putting this behind me." She ran her fingers over his banged up knuckles. "Just promise me you won't get yourself in trouble doing something silly like defending my honor."

"Don't make me promise something like that," Davis said, pulling her hand up to his lips and kissing it gently. "I'd hate to have to lie to you so soon after saying I love you."

Chapter Eighteen

She could smell his cologne before she could see him. And the Scotch he ended every night with lingered in the air as well. Caroline was right, Mick was probably drunk. It didn't happen often since he usually drank a steady stream of alcohol rather than overdoing it all at one time. But when he was stressed to the max he would put himself into a stupor. During their time together she'd made excuses to herself about his behavior. People didn't understand the pressure a man like Mick was under. When you reached a certain level of success you were expected to maintain that success. Every slip, every blunder, felt like the end of the world. Getting blackout drunk was just a way to blow off steam.

"Mick," Elaine said firmly as she rounded the back of his dented car. Because the world was full of irony, she realized he was standing on her curb. The place Davis had first found her when she'd run out of steam and had given up. "What are you doing here?"

"Elaine," he gulped, his hands twisted up in his hair as he eyed his car. Each dent seemed to be sending his blood pressure higher and higher. "You came? I've been calling you for days. I've been looking everywhere for you. I had your phone tracked last week but it was in New York. And you weren't. I called your father. He had no idea where you were.

Finally, I saw this picture of you posted online saying you were here. I got right in my car."

"Why?" she asked, not bothering to hide the quizzical smirk on her lips. "I didn't think we had much left to talk about. I don't appreciate you going secret agent and trying to track me down. That's an invasion of my privacy. You didn't need to bring my family into this. You've embarrassed me enough."

"What happened up there . . ." He rubbed the stubble on his cheek, and she realized how haggard he looked. In all the time she'd known him, even the years before they dated, there was never a day he'd gone without shaving. Wherever he went to get a shave they worked magic because his cheeks usually shimmered under the lights of the trading floor. Now his hair looked bushy and his lids drooped and fluttered randomly. "I still can't believe Elizabeth would do something like that. But so much of it was out of context. You didn't give me a chance to explain."

"There is nothing to explain, Mick. Nothing to forgive. It's behind us. Go back to New York. Go back to the firm. Just go." She stepped back as though everything was settled and he could leave now.

"I'm not leaving," he said, throwing up his arms and knocking himself off balance, the tell-tale sign that he'd had too much alcohol. Steading himself on the hood of his car he ground his teeth together. Fury rose in his face, and he unleashed his anger on the hood of his car in the way of two knuckle-breaking punches. But he was drunk enough not to wince.

"If it's about the car, it looks fine to drive. I'm

sure your insurance company can handle it there." Elaine leaned away but didn't give him the satisfaction of stepping back. He wouldn't hit her. Of all the things Mick was, an abuser of women he was not. If anything they'd shared was true, then the stories he told of his youth, and the horrors suffered at the hands of his father, must have been real. No one was a good enough actor to fake the pain he had in his eyes as he retold the nightmares.

"I'm not leaving without you," he said gently. There was a forced calm to his posture and expression. "Elaine, so much of what happened was just noise, but when I said I loved you, I meant it. I need you by my side in New York."

"You manipulated me to exploit my clients. If things would have gone any further, punitive action could have been taken. You were dating Elizabeth at the same time. I'm not sure you know what loves means at all." She propped her hands up on her hips and scolded him harshly. "You betrayed me, and now you expect me to leave with you?" The anger she thought was tethered to the ground was cut loose, and she was losing hold of it. Many hours had been spent imagining the moment she could fire every warranted bit of fury she could muster at Mick. But now, seeing him sway in the wind and lean on his dented car, it wasn't nearly as satisfying as she'd hoped.

Mick scoffed at her reluctance. "You plan to stay here? There isn't even a decent restaurant in this place. Where would you get sushi? I know you're mad, and you have every right to be. But I'll make it up to you. Just come back, and we'll start over. I have plenty of connections. I can get you another job. This is all going to blow over. I've already heard from firms who would like to hire you."

"And what? You and I just start dating again?" Elaine folded her arms across her chest and pursed her lips.

"Or we could get married," he sputtered out, inching closer, his hands pressed together in mock prayer. "Why not?"

"Why not?" she asked through a chuckle. "The list is literally too long to even try to explain. I'll just do the number one reason. You betrayed me."

"That's not fair," he asserted, swiping a hand through the air like he was cutting her argument down. "When we met I was very clear about the priority of my career. You understood that better than anyone I'd ever met before. You were equally driven and ambitious. We both danced around in the gray area here and there. But only because we knew we'd get better results. I hit a rough patch and I needed to fire up my portfolio some. You were a rock star in your role. I figured you could spare a couple of wins. I needed one badly."

"You should have talked to me," she huffed, putting her hands up stiffly as he approached. "Just go back on the curb, will you? Or better yet get in the car, sleep it off, and then drive home."

"I didn't have any feelings at all for Elizabeth. I wanted to try to get a meeting with her father. I was just making an in. You can understand that." He waved his hands animatedly as he pleaded his case.

"What is this really about?" Elaine asked,

knowing that familiar look on Mick's face. When he was mulling over an angle with a new client he'd always have the same expression. She'd just never noticed him using it on her before. Clearly she was the client he was trying to win over. But why?

"Come with me, and we can talk about it. We have a future together. You can't actually want to stay here," he said, gesturing around and rolling his eyes. "We can drive straight through the night and be at my place by morning."

"There is literally nothing you can say that would have me leaving with you tonight. I can't stress this enough. The answer is no." She shot him an unwavering stern look, still so shocked he believed she would be naïve enough to leave with him.

"And I'm not leaving without you," he said, taking another step forward.

"I'd bet against that," Davis said, stepping out of the shadows. "My money says we're going to do it her way."

"Oh, come on," Mick taunted. "The guy from the video? What, did you hire him to punch anyone you don't like? I saw what he did to those guys in the coffee shop. Back off, meathead."

"Don't," Elaine said, not sure which one of them she was directing it at. "Just stop. Mick, I am not going back to New York. That's all I have to say. You're too smart of a man to think I would."

"I'm spinning out," Mick cut in quickly, his voice cracking with emotion. "Lainie, please, you have to understand what's happened. Over the last few months, before all this, I was losing a lot of clients. I took some risks, and they didn't pan out. You know how that works."

"It happens, Mick," Elaine said, her voice noticeably softer now. "You're good at what you do. You'll bounce back."

"I won't. Not now. The reason I was meeting with some of your clients was because that was the only way I could stay afloat."

"You can have them all now," Elaine said with a breathy humorless laugh. "I'm not coming back so they are up for grabs. You've got a leg up on everyone, considering how I spilled my guts to you over all those dinners."

"You don't understand," Mick continued, his hands twisted back up in his hair again. "They know what happened. I can't even get a call back. Your clients loved you, and they think I hurt you."

"You did," she replied flatly.

"I know," he said, his voice rising with urgency. "But my own clients, they're leaving too. I'm losing everything."

"You should have thought of that," Elaine said, but the punch was gone from her voice now. She knew exactly what Mick's job meant to him, and it was falling apart. In her time in the industry she'd seen good people fall prey to drug addictions. Gambling. Rash decisions. A failed marriage. The same rush that drew them to the world of trading made them susceptible to the lure of easy money or a quick high.

"Come back with me, and take a job at another firm. I'll get you in. Let everyone see we're all right.

It's my only hope." Mick was running his words together like a freight train that couldn't be stopped.

"I'm sorry, Mick." She sighed, genuinely regretting the fact that she couldn't easily solve his problem. "I'm not going back to New York. I'm not working at another firm. I'm done. I'm at peace with it all."

"I completely understand you wanting to hurt me back," Mick countered, nodding his head as though he was agreeing with his own point. "But this is more than that. This would be ruining the rest of my life. You know that. If I don't get out of this tailspin, I'm done. No one understands better than you what that would do to me. I wouldn't survive it. I know you. You're too good of a person to let that happen. You have to help me. Even if I don't deserve it."

"I'm happy here," she replied, a thread of apology knitting her words together. "There is no chance I'm going to go commit to some job I don't want, just to help you. That's not a reasonable thing to ask of me."

"I think it's time to go," Davis said firmly, and Elaine felt the hair on the back of her neck stand up. The moment felt like a balloon already over inflated, yet someone continued to add more air, just daring it to burst. "She's not going to change her mind."

"You let this meathead talk for you?" Mick asked, his eyes never leaving Elaine. "That's not like you at all. No one was tougher than you. It's what made you so good at your job. It would be a waste to throw it away just because I screwed up. You have a really bright future."

"I do," she smiled, closing her eyes for a long beat and breathing in the sea air. "Right here. As a matter of fact, my future is as clear and bright as it's been in a long time. Indigo Bay is right where I belong. Nothing is going to change that. If you want, I can make some phone calls. I'll spread the word that there is no bad blood between us and that you're a solid choice for a broker. Both of those things are true. I'm not sitting in a corner somewhere crying over spilled milk, and you are still a powerhouse in the trading world. I would feel comfortable doing that for you."

Mick set his jaw tightly as though he was running out of patience. "That won't work. The rumors are flying. I need more than just a phone call. People need to see that we're really on the same side, and we've worked things out." Mick had his hands clamped together, pleading for her to reconsider.

"We haven't worked things out," Elaine refuted, her voice high and annoyed. "This is the most ridiculous thing I've ever heard. Do you realize five minutes ago you were proposing marriage solely based on the fact that you need me to ensure you don't lose your career? You need to take a hard look at your priorities."

"Marrying you would be the best choice I ever made," Mick corrected, his eyes growing watery with the shadow of emotions. "Forget for a second how badly I need you for my career, and remember what it was like on those late nights out on the boat. Remember how we talked for hours. I've never had that with anyone. I've played a lot of games in my life. Screwed people over. I never lost an ounce of sleep over it. But you, I'll never forgive myself for what I've done to you. We can make what we had real again. You're all I think about. You're all I want."

"Someone told me once," Elaine said, beginning in a whisper and then letting her voice grow, "the person who leaves you is always the one you long for. You think there's nothing that will make you feel better than getting them back. The rejection morphs itself into a desire to prove something and get them back. That's all that's happening here. What we had was not real. It couldn't be if you were trying to benefit from something that hurt me. And you wouldn't be asking me for things I can't give you."

"That should tell you how important this is to me," Mick said, lighting with recognition and snapping his fingers suddenly as though an idea had just come to him. "I know what we can do. The charity event. It's in a couple days. I know you RSVP'd. You could fly up, we could make the rounds. Everyone would be there. It's just one night."

"You say that like she owes you something," Davis bit out angrily. Elaine could practically feel him vibrating with the desire to forcibly remove Mick from town. She couldn't blame him. Mick was a pitbull. He set his sights on something and never settled until it went his way.

"Listen guy," Mick said, the arrogance instantly back in his voice, reminding Elaine how fake the sadness was. It was a faucet he could turn on and off. "I don't expect you to understand what's on the line here. What are you, a fisherman? A mechanic? You couldn't possibly know what it's like to handle what I do."

"You're right about that. Juggling women, stealing clients, that's all too much for me to handle. I prefer the simpler life of not being a steaming hot pile of garbage to people who don't deserve it. I don't need to drive a flashy car to make up for how disgusting my personality is. Unlike you, who dresses to show off how much money you make, my suit is tucked in the closet for special occasions like funerals. And if you don't get the hell out of here, maybe I'll be dusting it off to wear to yours."

"I'll think about it," Elaine interjected, and like a sail suddenly robbed of the steady wind, she could see Davis deflate and shrink back. "Just go sleep off whatever you've been drinking, and I'll talk to you tomorrow." She spun and headed away from both of them. Maybe one would follow, maybe both, maybe neither, but she couldn't stand in that bubble for another second and wait for it to pop.

Without another word Davis was on her heels, then jogged past her and opened the passenger door to his truck for her. As he moved in front of the truck to get back to the driver side she no longer had to wonder what he was thinking of this. The expression on his face was as clear as a cloudless summer sky. This was not what he signed up for.

Chapter Nineteen

"Sometimes not saying anything at all is worse," Elaine whispered, tracing her finger up and down the passenger window like a child passing the time on a long road trip.

"Worse than what?" Davis asked, his jaw clenched so tightly he thought his teeth might crack any second. But he wanted to keep his mouth shut. Nothing he'd say right now would be productive, and the last thing Elaine needed was another man demanding anything of her.

"Saying nothing is worse than telling me all the terrible things you're thinking. Just say what you want to say." She sighed. "I'm not an idiot; I can imagine how this all looks from the outside."

"I'm gonna stay out of it," Davis asserted, trying to convince himself he was capable of withholding his opinion. "You told him you were thinking about it, so think about it."

"But you have an opinion on the matter," she pressed, turning her body in the seat and staring at him. "You think I'm nuts for even considering it. That's only because you don't understand the nuance of the situation. Mick has spent his whole life trying to prove something to his family. It's very complicated, and his career is everything to him."

"I think my simple mind can deduce that from

the fact that he put his career above a relationship with a woman like you. He used you to get ahead. His career is important. Got it. It's in jeopardy now. But you lost your career all together."

"Actually, I've given that a lot more thought, and after talking to Mick tonight, I realized I was overreacting. There are firms I could get back into if I wanted to, and my clients would likely be sympathetic to my situation. I could build my reputation back up. I let anxiety get in my head. It was actually good to hear him say that."

"Sounds like you've got it all planned out then," Davis snapped, hating the petty shots he was taking but feeling unable to hold them back. He was wounded, and there was no denying the pain.

"I'm not saying I want to take a job at those firms. I'm saying I could, and there is something very liberating about that for me. It means being in Indigo Bay is a choice, not a sentence for a crime I committed. But for Mick, it'll be different. If he doesn't get out of this spiral, he might not recover, and his future is shot. I can't live with that. One night in New York could solve most of his problems. I owe—"

"Please don't even finish that sentence. You don't owe him a night. You don't owe him a day; you don't owe him a second. He brought this on himself and he should have to deal with the consequences."

"I wish you would see this for what it is," Elaine pleaded. "I don't want to go back to work. I don't want to be with Mick. I want to be here with you. I'd just like to do it without all the baggage. The reason

Mick had been successful is because he doesn't quit. If I don't agree to help him now, he'll never stop. He's relentless when it comes to his future."

"Give me five minutes alone with him, and I'll show you how quick he'll leave you alone and for good. I don't care if you want to go to New York with him, but I'm not going to sit around and pretend you're going because you have no choice or because you think it's a debt you should pay. You're an adult. You don't owe me anything, but at least be honest with yourself."

"Thanks," she said. "This is really productive. What a great night this turned into."

"The cabin's repaired. That's what Caroline said. Dallas had the roof fixed." Davis felt like he was spitting nails rather than talking, and judging by the look on her face, Elaine was the target getting pelted.

"Yeah, I think that's a good idea. Unless you have anything else to say. If you have anything else that might help." She looked at him with such desperation he felt like the air was leaving the truck.

There were a thousand things Davis wanted to say. He'd bungled this, and he was chasing her off like a fool. But words were clay he couldn't mold into anything of substance. They just sat like lumps in his throat. Instead he and Elaine remained in complete and suffocating silence right up until the moment she got back to her car and drove away. The red taillights faded into the darkness as she disappeared, dragging his heart behind like tin cans on a newlywed's car.

Chapter Twenty

"You're an idiot," Caroline said, her voice layered with disappointed as she filled Davis's coffee mug "You couldn't have handled that any worse. Complete incompetence of all things involving the heart. Is that what you're going for, first place in failure?"

"Are you done?" Davis asked, spooning some sugar into his mug and mixing it as though he were creating an elixir that might heal him.

"Like a squirrel trying to do math. Or a rock trying to run a marathon. You are hopeless, and every time you look like maybe you're going to get out of your own way . . . boom. You do something like this. I don't know what to do with you."

"Give him a break," Dallas said, strolling through the door, looking a little ragged. His T-shirt was wrinkled and his baseball hat was pulled low over his eyes. "It's been a long night."

"I haven't even begun with you yet," Caroline scolded, gesturing for her son to sit as though the booth was a time out chair for a toddler. "But let me finish with him first. You don't get to tell a girl what she should be doing. If she's got something to work out, you need to trust her." Caroline was pacing around wiping already clean tables and pushing in chairs another fraction of an inch. "Who do you think you are?"

"I love her," Davis replied flatly. "Maybe I'm an idiot. Maybe I'm screwing it all up. I'm not sure. But what I do know is I'm not getting involved with another woman who doesn't know what she wants in life. I know where I want to be and what kind of life I want. Maybe I figured it out earlier than most. If she's in a state of flux, I'm not going through it again. If she needs time to figure out her stuff, then she can take that time. But she can do it on her own."

"You're stubborn as a mule," Dallas said, stealing away the bowl of sugar packets and looking pitifully at his mother for a cup of coffee. "But I admire your dedication to your own foolishness. It's impressive."

"Thanks," Davis said, taking a long sip of his coffee to rub in the fact that at least he'd been given that. "I knew I could count on you two to make me feel better."

"We're your friends," Caroline sighed, tossing the towel in her hand over her shoulder and propping her hands on her hips. "We're not meant to make you *feel better*. We're meant to help you *be better*. And for the last few years we've been failing you. I want you to think long and hard about this opportunity you have with Elaine. Stop pretending the ball is in her court and start realizing you've both got the control in this situation. No one is perfectly right or perfectly wrong. And don't compare this to what happened with Julie. It's light years different. You're different. Dallas and I, along with loads of other people in this town, want to see you happy. Quit making that so hard."

"What do you propose I do?" Davis asked, genuinely unsure of how Caroline saw this thing turning out well. "She's going to go to New York, to this charity event just to help a guy who doesn't deserve it. Her flight already took off. There's no running through the airport and chasing her down."

"What a terribly generous thing for her to do," Dallas laughed cynically. "I've always hated that quality in people. Loyalty. Selflessness. It's exhausting to be around people willing to do something nice even when it puts their own life in turmoil."

"When you put it that way," Davis grunted, sliding out of the booth and heading for the door. "I need some time to think. Caroline give this poor guy a cup of coffee, he's fresh out of jail."

Caroline hummed her disappointment. "He's on punishment." She closed in on Davis before he could reach the door and whispered her last bit of advice "The happiest I've seen you in a long time was sitting across from Elaine every morning. Laughing and sipping your coffee. Go think. Go be alone. But when you close your eyes if she's the one you see, if she's what makes your heart smile, then fix this fast."

"Night," Davis said, halfway out the door as her words chased him out. He'd been in moments like this before. And one thing he'd learned about loving a woman who needed room to run was that his selfishness had been far more of a factor than the circumstances he'd kept blaming. It was time for him to either tame the beast within, or come to terms with the fact that his life would always bring him to this very moment. Like a book you had to keep reading until you understood what you were meant to learn, his eyes were finally starting to open.

Chapter Twenty-One

Elaine struggled to zip her favorite black cocktail dress. After a couple weeks in Indigo Bay, eating all that cobbler, she was lucky it still fit well enough to wear tonight. Her long hair was resting on her shoulders, curled into symmetrical coils that framed her face. She'd done all her normal primping, but as she passed the mirror she felt like something was missing. Earrings. Check. Lipstick applied. Check. Her eyeliner was straight. She stared hard until she realized it was her smile. She hadn't smiled since Davis dropped her off at her car that night and she sped away without another word.

Now as her heart thudded in her chest, the afternoon having too quickly turned to night, she wondered if she'd made the right choice. The charity event would be held downstairs so having a room in the hotel made things easier. In reality, she just hadn't wanted to spend the night alone in her apartment. Something about being at the hotel made everything feel less permanent. Less real.

Even hiding in the hotel, questions swirled in her mind. Was it principles that had her returning to New York? Was it fear? Fear of how quickly and resolutely she'd fallen for Davis? The questions spun, but the answers never surfaced.

A light knock on her door sent her jumping. She

stepped back from her own reflection and resolved that maybe her smile might be elusive for a little while.

"Elaine, it's me," Mick said through the door, his voice far more steady than the last time they'd spoken.

Her raw nerves felt like another round of sandpaper had been unleashed on them as she swung the door open and glared at him. There he was standing right in front of her like a bashful fool. "I told you I'd meet you downstairs. This is not going to work if you keep finding new ways to piss me off. The whole point was for me to show people I'm fine, and there is no bad blood between us. Keep messing with my boundaries and there may be actual blood between us. Yours."

"I know, but I was ready early, and I thought I'd come see how you were doing. Maybe we could walk down together." He reached out a hand, his expensive gold watch catching the light. She'd seen him in a tux a few times before, but tonight it seemed ill fitting. The magic that had once buzzed between them had evaporated.

"I'm not here to pretend we're still together," she corrected. "I'm fine with showing everyone how fine I am, but I'm not letting you parade me around like we're dating. That's where I draw the line."

Mick pulled his hand back as though she'd slapped it, tucking it quickly into his pocket. "That's not it at all. I just figured, at one point in time you and I had a lot of fun together. We really understood each other. I miss that. I hoped we could just catch up a little, now that things have settled down. It was so tense in Indigo Beach."

"Indigo Bay," Elaine corrected as though the distinction was extremely important.

"Right," he nodded. "But can you admit we used to be good together?"

"We did have fun," she conceded. "But it was pretend. You know that."

"That's not how I see it, Lainie," he said, tilting his head in that familiar way and turning up half his face in a smile. She could smack herself for all the times she fell for his charm. His tricks. "I'm sorry. I'm not trying to make you uncomfortable. I just had to tell you that your showing up here means everything to me. It's a testament to the kind of person you are. To the kind of person I lost."

"You didn't lose me, Mick," she said flatly. "I'm not a set of keys you misplaced. I'm a person you chose to use. I'm here now to try to put it all behind me. I'd prefer to meet you downstairs like we originally discussed." Elaine folded her arms across her chest and waited for him to go.

"Of course," he nodded and shuffled backward. "Sorry again."

When he rounded the corner toward the elevator Elaine closed the door and drew in a deep breath. She'd been rattled by his deception, and the more time she had to reflect on it the more it chilled her to the core. A smart woman like her should certainly have been able to see through a man with bad intentions. Somehow though, Mick had snowballed her. So had Elizabeth. Did that mean her judgment was terrible. Could her impression and feelings for Davis be trusted?

Another small knock on the door sent Elaine into a near rage. If this was how Mick was going to spend his time tonight, she'd bail on this whole thing.

"I told you already, Mick, to go downstairs," she said as she pulled the door open to find Davis standing there, a perfectly fitted tuxedo on and a single red rose in his hand.

"Davis," she choked out, a hand flying up to her heart. "What are you doing here? How did you—?"

"I'm glad to hear you're sending men away from your hotel room door, but I hope to break the trend." His smile was wide but nervous.

"Come in," she said, yanking his sleeve. "Get in here."

"I thought of something to say," he offered, still standing stiffly by the door, but at least inside the room now. "I thought of about a thousand things to say actually, but I know you don't have that kind of time."

"I'll make time," she smiled, her eyes dampening. "I have things I need to say too. But you first."

"OK." He drew in a deep breath and closed his eyes for an extra beat. "I'm not sure where to start, but I just want you to know that I see things clearly now. You asked me to see this for what it is, and I can. I realize what is happening tonight. You aren't going on a date with your ex. You are walking into a lion's den to help someone who, on all accounts, wasn't worthy of your help. You're walking into a room full of people who laughed at you, or yelled at you, or intentionally tried to hurt you. Or, worse than that, a room full of people who pity you. I don't know that I could do what you're doing. It doesn't make you weak, it makes you intensely strong. The reasons you're here tonight are the reasons you were so easy to fall in love with."

She felt the tears that had welled in her eyes spill over as he handed her the rose and touched her cheek gently. "Davis, I'm not even sure I can walk in there tonight," she admitted. "I thought I could. But I have no idea what people are going to say, how they'll react. I'm second-guessing myself."

He took her hand and pulled her in close. "Whatever you want, I've got your back. You want me to stay out of it, then forget I rented this tux and go in there on your own. If you want me by your side, I'll be your shadow all night. Or if you want to run out of here right now and go eat hot dogs off a street cart in these fancy clothes, we can do that too. Whatever you want."

"Option B," she smiled, raising up on her tiptoes to kiss him. "I don't want to go down there and put on a show, pretend I'm happy. So the best thing I can do is show up with someone who actually makes me happy."

"Does that ruin Mick's plan?" Davis asked, looking only mildly concerned with that idea.

"He gets what he wants. Nothing can show them how little effect he had on me more than what a profound effect you have on me. I know if we walk in there together, I can do this." She paused and stared him straight in the eyes, longing for something important. "You need to promise not to hit anyone."

"Because it's a fancy affair?" Davis asked, taking a step back and straightening his bow tie with sarcastic haughtiness.

"No, because the people around here have million dollar lawyers, and I'd prefer if you and I were heading back to Indigo Bay in the morning and not to your court hearing. I'm being serious. No matter what happens down there, don't hit anyone."

"I promise," Davis assured her. "I won't make things more complicated for you just because I want to bash a jerk's face in."

"And that means a lot to me," she joked, slipping her arm in his and leaning on him. "Now don't let me go until it's time to leave there tonight."

"How about I don't let you go ever," he asked, tightening his bicep and looking down at her lovingly.

"Deal."

Chapter Twenty-Two

It was about exactly as stuffy an event as Davis had imagined. The appetizers were small and the tablecloths were long. Perfume and cologne mingled together in a cloud he couldn't seem to avoid, no matter where he stepped. Elaine started out tense, shaking as she pressed against him, but now seemed better.

Their arms weren't locked together anymore because so many familiar faces wanted to offer her hugs and handshakes. It was all kind words and condolences that Elaine met with dismissal and laughter. "I don't rattle easily," she lied and waved their pity off. "I'm actually thrilled to be starting a new chapter of my life. Sometime you need something to bump you out of an old rut."

Her attitude and smile were widely accepted and turned quickly to relief on the faces of her old coworkers and clients. Every chance she had, Davis was introduced as her boyfriend and the man who'd swept her away to a beach town and convinced her to stay.

"So you aren't coming back to the industry? I know a CEO interested in meeting with you. I had hoped to work with you again." The offers and disappointments all blurred together, there were so many.

"I'll be in Indigo Bay," she replied. "My toes in the sand and the sun on my face. I've got everything I need. I'm done with this wild pace. Life is too short."

Everything seemed to be going her way as the hours ticked by and the event began to draw to a close.

"Lainie," Mick called, and she placed her champagne down on a passing tray. "I was hoping to catch you." His eyes landed on Davis, and shock spread across his face. "Oh, you're here."

"I am," Davis replied flatly, but cleared his throat as a small group of people seemed to gather around to watch what might happen. "I wouldn't miss a chance to escort a woman like Elaine to such a beautiful event."

"Escort is the key word," a shrill and unfamiliar voice chimed in. A tall redhead, who was too much collarbone and not enough curves, elbowed her way to them.

"Elizabeth," Mick said in a scolding tone but Elaine jumped in.

"How are you, Elizabeth?" Elaine asked, coolly.

"This guy must be an escort. Look at him. Do those pants rip away when the music starts playing? How much did he cost you to put on this show?"

"What show?" Elaine asked, twisting her face up in annoyance.

"Coming here with this guy on your arm like everything is all right. You got fired. You don't even belong here."

"We're raising money for the children's hospital, Elizabeth," she countered. "I think we can all put petty disagreements aside and rally behind the cause."

Nicely played. She would not sink to Elizabeth's level, and in the process make the girl look like more of a fool than she already had herself.

"Is there a problem here?" a voice, rattling with old age, asked. A hunchbacked woman in a gold sequined dress and shawl approached, looking stern.

"Mrs. Wilmington," Elaine sang happily as she closed the gap between them and kissed the old woman on the cheek. "How are you?"

"I'm so glad you came, dear. I'm well. I wanted to call you, but I thought maybe you would like some space. I just got word that you joined us tonight, and I was anxious to come see you. Tell me now, dear, what is happening?"

"Nothing at all, Mrs. Wilmington. Davis and I were just getting ready to leave."

"I wish you'd rethink that," the old woman said, holding Elaine's forearm for support. "I would like some of your time to discuss a few matters."

"Of course," Elaine agreed. "Shall we sit?"

"Why would anyone want your advice?" Elizabeth cackled. "The old coot must not have the internet. Maybe she's the only one on earth who hasn't seen what an idiot you are. This guy is someone she hired to pretend to be her date," Elizabeth said loudly and slow as if the old woman needed the accommodation of both.

"Why is this girl yelling at me?" Mrs. Wilmington asked no one in particular, and the crowd chuckled. "Is it that she doesn't know who I am, or she thinks I don't know who she is? Because I certainly do know."

"Excuse me?" Elizabeth gasped. "I'm just trying to warn you. Elaine here did less than reputable things to get ahead. If you are going to ask her business questions, you might want to reconsider. I took over her job, I'd be much more suitable."

"The only thing you're suitable for," Mrs. Wilmington replied so coolly it sounded like the chorus of a song, "is following my dogs around, waiting to fill some plastic bags with their messes. Outside of that, I can't think of a single use for you."

Elaine, and nearly everyone else, broke out into a hearty laugh as Elizabeth's freckles faded into her fully red face. "Some old rich hag isn't going to stand here with this loser and tell me where I belong. Do you know who my father is?"

"I do." Mrs. Wilmington laughed. "We've done business together for almost forty years. I was one of the first investors in his company. We have lunch once a month. If he heard you just called me an old hag, I'd bet my summer house in the mountains you'd be cut off faster than a dead fish on the line."

"Daddy would never cut me off," Elizabeth scoffed. "You're senile."

"Elaine dear," Mrs. Wilmington said sweetly. "Can you get my phone out of my purse? I'd like to make a call and see which one of us is right."

"I wouldn't waste your time, Mrs. Wilmington," Elaine said, patting the old woman's hand. "Elizabeth is her own worst enemy. We don't have to knock her down a few pegs; she'll do that on her own soon enough."

"Ladies," Mick cut in like he'd been timing an entry point into a jump rope competition. "I know that things between us—"

"Nope," Elaine said sharply. "There were no things between us," she corrected, gesturing between the three of them. "There is nothing there to discuss. I'm going to chat with Mrs. Wilmington, if you will excuse me."

"I'm going to put in a higher bid for your guy," Elizabeth said, inching closer to Davis. "He won't be here when you get back."

With that Elaine felt a lava of anger rise, volcano style, from her toes to her face. "Back off," she asserted, handing Mrs. Wilmington's needed support over to Davis and closing in on Elizabeth. "You don't have any idea what you're talking about, and I'd appreciate it if you left."

The crowd rumbled its agreement, and that seemed to set Elizabeth over the edge. Not being liked by the masses clearly did not sit well with her. "Make me," she mouthed angrily.

"I'm not going to hit you," Elaine sneered. "We aren't children."

"I'm going to take everything from you. What's the name of that stupid town you ended up in? Indigo Bay? I'll have my father flatten it, and turn it into a shopping strip. I'll take him. I'll take whatever you have left."

"Hit her," Mrs. Wilmington bit out, and Elaine couldn't hold back her laughter. "Don't laugh, whack her."

"Mrs. Wilmington, I'm not going to—" The ice

cold contents of a glass splashed across Elaine's face and cut her words short. That shrew had just tossed a drink in her face. She blinked away the droplets and licked the champagne from her lips.

"I'm the bigger person here," Elaine ground out and was met with a roll from Elizabeth's cloudy gray eyes. "I mean I'm literally bigger than you," she shouted, sweeping a leg out from under Elizabeth and sending her to the ground. She landed with a thud, her emerald green dress ripping at the seam, and her high heels flying off. "Get up and I will make you wish you hadn't."

A hardy round of applause broke out from the small group surrounding them, and Elaine positioned Mrs. Wilmington's shaky arm back on hers. "Davis, would you like to join us while we chat?" Elaine asked so calmly Davis could hardly believe what he'd just seen.

"Sure," he croaked out, lending his arm to Mrs. Wilmington's other side and smiling warmly when she took it.

"You're a better woman than I am," Mrs. Wilmington offered. "I'd have at least stomped on her a few times while she was down there."

Chapter Twenty-Three

The waves were calm that morning, and Elaine could hear the gulls more clearly than usual.

"Not a bad place to wake up," Davis said, handing her a mug of hot coffee. "It never gets old."

"There is nothing like the sea," she said, slipping her arm around his waist and breathing in the scent of the strong coffee and his familiar skin. "There is nothing like being here with you."

"I was thinking we could do something together today," he began, sipping on his coffee and making her wait for more details. "The cottage, it doesn't look right just plain old white. Maybe we could go into town and pick a color we both like and give it a fresh coat."

"That would be nice," she said, nuzzling against him. "Do we have time for cobbler first?"

"There is always time for cobbler," he assured her as the sun finally broke free of the horizon. "I was thinking after we paint the cottage we could have a party."

"Sure," she said, shrugging as he led her back up the dunes to the house. "Dinner?"

"I was thinking an engagement party," he said, not turning around to see her expression. But she could tell the corners of his mouth had risen nearly to his ears. "You know, only if you say yes." He turned suddenly and knelt, the motion sending her hands flying to her mouth in shock.

"Davis, are you serious?"

"Because of you, I'm serious. And I'm silly. And I'm tired, and I've got all the energy in the world. I'm everything, every minute of the day because I found you. It's like you turned the switch on in my life."

"Yes," she said, reluctantly dropping her shaking hand down so he could slide the diamond ring on her finger. "I'll marry you."

"Then we better get cooking," he said, pulling her into his arms, lifting her high, and spinning her around. "There are two things on the menu tonight," he said, dropping her down and kissing her cheek softly.

"Mashed potatoes and cake?" she asked, her cheeks aching from her wide smile.

"And when people ask why, we'll tell them it's because that's what we ate the night I fell in love with you," Davis explained. "Even though it's not the same night you fell in love with me."

"If we want to show everyone the moment I fell in love with you," she said, running her hands through his hair and looking deeply in his eyes, "we'll have to go back to that curb you found me on. Because the second you told me everything was going to be all right, for the first time in a long time I believed it. I knew you wouldn't stop until it was. And I knew I loved you right then and there."

"So mashed potatoes and cake on the curb," he announced as he pulled her in toward the house. "But that doesn't sound New York City kind of fancy."

"No," she said, rolling her eyes. "It sounds perfect."

The End

Books by Danielle Stewart

Piper Anderson Series

Book 1: Chasing Justice
Book 2: Cutting Ties
Book 3: Changing Fate
Book 4: Finding Freedom
Book 5: Settling Scores
Book 6: Battling Destiny
Book 7: Chris & Sydney Collection – Choosing Christmas & Saving Love
Betty's Journal - Bonus Material (suggested to be read after Book 4 to avoid spoilers)

Edenville Series – A Piper Anderson Spin Off

Book 1: Flowers in the Snow
Book 2: Kiss in the Wind
Book 3: Stars in a Bottle

Piper Anderson Legacy Mystery

Book 1: Three Seconds To Rush
Book 2: Just for a Heartbeat

The Clover Series

Hearts of Clover - Novella & Book 2: (Half My Heart & Change My Heart)
Book 3: All My Heart
Book 4: Facing Home

Rough Waters Series

Book 1: The Goodbye Storm
Book 2: The Runaway Storm
Book 3: The Rising Storm

Midnight Magic Series

Amelia

The Barrington Billionaires Series

Book 1: Fierce Love
Book 2: Wild Eyes
Book 3: Crazy Nights

Author Information

One random newsletter subscriber will be chosen every month this year. The chosen subscriber will receive a $25 eGift Card! Sign up today by visiting www.authordaniellestewart.com

Author Contact:
Website: AuthorDanielleStewart.com

Email: AuthorDanielleStewart@Gmail.com

Facebook: Author Danielle Stewart

Twitter: @DStewartAuthor

Made in United States
Orlando, FL
21 February 2022

15039641R00093